NO LONG
SEATTLE PUBLIC LIBRARY

Her mama let her spend all kinds of time with me, and Ivy came to my house after school nine days out of ten. I hardly went back to her place after that first time. Ivy didn't ask, and I was just as glad.

I was amazed at how we liked all the same things: pepperoni pizza, RC Cola, swimming, singing, and playing Monopoly. We both wanted a pair of in-line roller skates but didn't think we'd ever get them. Also, neither one of us was exactly popular in school. Ivy was too quiet and wary, and I was too flat-out strange. But we didn't care, we had each other.

We'd talk and talk—mostly about the future. I'd keep on at the farm as my folks did, only I wanted to have a horse to ride around, too. Ivy wanted to be a ballet dancer, and have a dog, and maybe be a famous movie director one day.

After a while we'd go play with the cats, or swing on the tire swing, or build forts out of hay bales up in the mow and pretend we were Wild West cowboys or Cherokee Indians. Sometimes we pretended we were orphan princesses running a great kingdom together. Other times we just hiked back along the lane to the woods to see what we could see.

OTHER BOOKS YOU MAY ENJOY

PRAIRIE EVERS

ellen airgood

PUFFIN BOOKS
An Imprint of Penguin Group (USA)

For my mother,
Anita Ann Airgood,
the backbone of my happy childhood.

PUFFIN BOOKS
Published by the Penguin Group
Penguin Group (USA) LLC
375 Hudson Street
New York, New York 10014

USA * Canada * UK * Ireland * Australia
New Zealand * India * South Africa * China

penguin.com
A Penguin Random House Company

First published in the United States of America by Nancy Paulsen Books,
an imprint of Penguin Young Readers Group, 2012
Published by Puffin Books, an imprint of Penguin Young Readers Group, 2014

Copyright © 2012 by Ellen Airgood

Penguin supports copyright. Copyright fuels creativity, encourages diverse voices, promotes
free speech, and creates a vibrant culture. Thank you for buying an authorized edition of this
book and for complying with copyright laws by not reproducing, scanning, or distributing any
part of it in any form without permission. You are supporting writers and allowing Penguin to
continue to publish books for every reader.

THE LIBRARY OF CONGRESS HAS CATALOGED THE NANCY PAULSEN BOOKS EDITION AS FOLLOWS:
Airgood, Ellen.
Prairie Evers / Ellen Airgood.
p. cm.
Summary: "Ten-year-old Prairie is happy being home-schooled and raising her flock of chickens, so transferring to regular school is a big change, but fortunately she meets a wonderful
friend"—Provided by publisher.
ISBN 978-0-399-25691-2 (hardcover)
[1. Farm life—New York (State)—Fiction. 2. Family life—New York (State)—Fiction.
3. Chickens—Fiction. 4. Schools—Fiction. 5. Friendship—Fiction.
6. Grandmothers—Fiction. 7. New Paltz (N.Y.)—Fiction.] I. Title.
PZ7.P28114Pr 2012 [Fic]—dc23
2011046789

Puffin Books ISBN 978-0-14-242668-5

Printed in the United States of America

7 9 10 8

CONTENTS

THE OLD SHOE

Just exactly one year ago, right after midnight on New Year's Eve, my grammy told me, "Prairie, I have ushered in the new year with you, and that is all I can do. A body as old as me has only got so much time left. I've got to go home."

I stared at her, my hand hanging above the Monopoly board. I was the top hat and Grammy was the old shoe. Those are the pieces we always chose. I'd thought she seemed a little distracted— she let Reading Railroad go without a peep, and normally Grammy wouldn't let a railroad go for anything—but I'd put it down to the lateness of the hour. The big hand on the kitchen clock had already clicked past twelve with a little hop like it always does, and Mama and Daddy had tromped off to bed the very next instant. So it was just me and Grammy at the table, drinking RC Colas and playing Monopoly while outside the wind gnawed at the corners of the house and sent darts of cold in at the windows.

"You are now ten years of age. You're well grown and have your mama and daddy to look after you. I'm going back to North Carolina where I belong."

I could not believe what I was hearing. "But we just *got* here." I didn't feel that way really. We'd lived in New York State for three months so far and it already felt like a hundred years to me, but I had to try and talk her out of this idea any way I could.

"I'm sorry, child."

"You *can't* go. Where would you live?" Mama and Daddy sold our house on Peabody Mountain when we left North Carolina, and Grammy had always lived with us.

"I'll go to Vine's Cove. My roots are there, and here I'm withering like a tree yanked out of the earth."

I thought, You are my earth. How will I grow up any more without you?

Grammy read my thoughts plain. "You'll do all right. You have a good mama and daddy to help you along. But this life up north in New York State is not for me."

"It's not for me either," I declared. "I'll go with you."

I felt a great gust of relief at that idea. Of course it was the answer. Vine's Cove was the next closest thing to home, after Peabody Mountain. Grammy's brother, Great-Uncle Tecumseh Vine, lived there, and I liked him. He lived way back in the mountainy woods in the cabin he was born in, a little old shack made of pine logs and plank floors. It didn't look like much, but it had withstood the test of time for over one hundred years. That's what Grammy always said anyway.

"You can't do that, child. You have to stay here with your mama and daddy."

"Maybe Mama and Daddy will move back too, if we're there."

"Prairie, child, use your head. You know they've just got started here. You know they could never get this much land down home. It's only because your mama's folks passed on to their greater reward that they've got this now."

"Well, they may've gone on to their greater reward, but it hasn't turned out so good for me," I muttered. Then I ducked my head and hoped the Lord would not strike me down. Mama's folks had perished in a car accident, and it was very tragic. I knew that the way you know something in your head, but I always felt guilty I didn't feel it more in my heart. But the thing was, I never really knew them. They never got down to North Carolina and we never got up to New York State. Until now.

"Prairie, Prairie," Grammy said, sounding sorrowful.

"But I don't like it here. If you're going home, I'm going too."

"You can't."

"But—"

"You're young, you'll adjust. But my heart is broke, you see. I miss the smell of the mountains too much."

"It smells like mountains here." I couldn't believe I was defending this place, but it was true. It did smell like mountains here, a little different from home but still mountains—rocky and mossy and shadowy and good. If that was her reason for going, I couldn't let her get away with it.

Grammy gave me a sad, crinkly smile. "The plain fact is, I'm feeling old. My bones ache and my eyes are dim and my grinders have become few." She meant that she didn't have many of her own teeth left. She was grinning to take the sting out of all this, but it didn't work.

"Grammy."

"I'm not going to kick the bucket tomorrow. But I can't live the last of my life up here, so far from the sights and sounds I grew up with. I expected I could make this change but I cannot. My heart has turned toward home and I have got to follow. I'm sorry."

"But who will teach me?" I cried, my last stab at changing her mind.

"Your mama and daddy will finish out this school year." There was something odd about the way she said it, something unfinished that made me uneasy for a moment, but I didn't pay attention. My heart was so sad and surprised by what she was saying, I couldn't think straight.

Grammy frowned and smooched her lips out and frowned some more—it was to keep any tears from escaping, I knew—and then she rolled the dice and marched the old shoe down the board three spaces. She said, "Look there now, I've landed on your railroad. What is it that I owe you?"

I wanted to say "nothing" and shove away from the table and go to bed without another word. But I didn't. I stared at the board for a long time and then I said, "It is twenty-five dollars," as she well knew, being the railroad magnate that she was.

GOOD-BYE

A few days later we went to the bus station with Grammy and waved her away. I struggled mightily, but I couldn't keep from crying. My heart was cracking into a million pieces, and no matter how broken it got, it kept on breaking.

We went back to the house—I couldn't think of it as home yet—and Mama fixed lunch. I poked at my macaroni and cheese, which Mama makes all cheesy and bubbly and crunchy on top. Normally it's one of my favorite meals, but I didn't have any appetite. I went to my room and crawled under the covers.

Mama came and looked in on me after a while. "How are you holding up?"

"I hate it here. I want to go home."

Mama sat on the edge of my bed and patted my shoulder. "This was my room, you know," she said after a while. "I always liked that window that looks east. I liked to watch the sun rise. I felt like I was the first one seeing the world get born every day."

I sighed, but I liked knowing Mama and I felt the same about that window. The first thing I did every day back at home was look outside. I'd check on the weather and see the tangle of honeysuckle scrambling up the barn wall, the dark, quiet clump of rhododendron standing by the well house, the slender branches of the redbud tree etched against the mountainside. Here the view was different—there was a big hemlock tree giving the sky a sharp poke, an old chicken coop whose boards were as gray as a rainy day, a barn and some sheds and a meadow rolling slowly down the hill toward town—but it gave me the same good feeling to survey the world from up on high first thing.

"It's a good house," Mama said. "I hope you'll like it better here one day."

That made me feel like crying all over again. It sounded so final.

The house was a little old farmhouse with steep, narrow stairs to the second floor, where there were two bedrooms tucked up under the eaves, one small and the other one, where Grammy had slept, smaller yet. It had a shady screened-in porch along the front and a big kitchen in the back with a potbelly stove in the center of the room. Outside there was the chicken coop, a falling-down shed and a standing-up one, a little barn with a steep, pointy roof, and about a hundred acres of gardens and berry patches Mama and Daddy had all kinds of plans for. Well, not a hundred acres really, but plenty. There was a big grassy meadow on the east side of the property and a craggy rock cliff along the west. The farm sat at the end of a dead-end dirt road that ran alongside a chunk of the Shawangunk Mountains, and if you couldn't be at home in North Carolina, it was probably the next best thing. The house was homey and cozy even though the wind did whistle in at the windows some, and I had been getting just a little bit used to it all when Grammy took off and left me.

"It'll be too quiet up here now. Grammy and I always talked at night."

"I know you did."

"Every night we gave everything a good going over. What we saw on our walks and how the garden was doing and my lessons and everything. And she always read to me. It'll be too lonely. I won't be able to sleep."

Mama stroked a lock of my hair and said, "Well, Daddy and I can read to you if you want. And you can read to yourself, too."

"I know." It would be too mean to say it wouldn't be the same. I got along with my mama and daddy like bread and butter. But Grammy wasn't just my grammy. She was my teacher and my best friend too. For my whole life I'd been tagging after her, doing everything she did. We were always investigating. If we were outdoors, it was birds and trees and plants and bugs and the shape of clouds. Inside, it was the history of plumbing and where cocoa came from and how to make some crazy thing like eggs Benedict. Once, we even made our own marshmallows, or we tried anyway.

Grammy was always curious about things, and failing in an endeavor never got her down long. That was life, she said: noticing and trying. You didn't have to succeed as long as you put your back into the effort. Everything gave her an idea about something else—something she had read or seen—and we were constantly looking further into the matter. There were so many books in our house, we didn't even try to move them all north. Boxes and boxes got packed away and stowed in Great-Uncle Tecumseh's shed, which I knew fretted Grammy something awful. She feared the damp would get into them and the mice would chew their pages despite the mothballs she sprinkled all around. I was convinced that was half the reason she headed back home.

"It's like there's a ghost," I told Mama, but it wasn't like that really. It was like there was a great echoing emptiness that scared me more than any ghost ever could.

"I know. We'll miss her too." Mama kept on patting my shoulder, and after a while I felt a tiny bit less woeful.

"I'm hungry," I said.

"I could heat up some of the leftover macaroni and cheese."

I sighed. Then I said, "Okay." I followed Mama back down to the kitchen and sat in the rocker right close to the potbelly stove while she heated my lunch back up. I felt like an invalid who had only just begun to recover from a terrible flu.

OH GLORY, HOW HAPPY I AM

That first while after Grammy left, I was always closing my eyes and pretending she was just over in the next room. Maybe she was canning tomatoes, or checking the lessons she gave me, or picking out a little tune on her banjo. Whatever she was doing, she was always singing. In my mind I could hear her voice, all wavery and plain, belting out "Oh Glory, How Happy I Am" like there was no tomorrow. She always said that song just made a person feel better.

After she left, I tried singing "Oh Glory, How Happy I Am." I never could remember the rest of the words, but even just that one line did make me feel better. But only for a little while. Pretty soon I'd go back to being lonesome again.

Some of that lonesome time I spent out in the chicken coop that I could see from my bedroom window. It was like a little house of my own, a secret place I could go to think. I'd sit hunched in the corner, bundled up in my winter clothes but still chilled to the bone, missing Grammy and Peabody Mountain and even the neighbor lady's mob of kids who used to drive me wild with all their shouting. I'd daydream I had a twin sister to keep me company or that Mama and Daddy had announced we were moving back home. But I knew that wasn't going to happen.

After a while I got the idea that it'd be nice to have something living in that henhouse, something like a chicken. The minute I thought of it, I knew it was right. I could see the flock of hens bustling around the yard, cheering me up. Then I imagined a big beautiful rooster, his head tipped back while he crowed.

I brought my idea up with Mama and Daddy at breakfast one morning.

"Chickens!" Mama said, like she had never heard of such an animal before.

Daddy leveled a doubtful look at me. "What in the world made you think of that?"

"I like the looks of them. They have those funny bodies,

14

all round and fat, and then those skinny little heads up top. I think it'd be fun to have a bunch of them running around. That coop out back is what gave me the idea."

Mama and Daddy were still looking at me kind of doubtful, so I said, "I think it'd be interesting." Finding things interesting is highly regarded in my family.

I gave the egg Mama had fried for me a poke while I thought how else to convince them. The egg was done just the way I liked it, runny in the middle with crispy edges, but it was store bought, you could tell. The yolk was pale and weak. "If we had our own chickens, we could have good strong yellow eggs like Mrs. Perkins raised back home. And maybe I could sell the eggs like she did."

Daddy nodded, real slow. He looked over at Mama, who shrugged and raised her eyebrows. And he said, "Well then, you go on and give it a try. If you're sure."

"I am! So now what?" I looked at them expectantly. "Did you have chickens growing up, Mama? Do you know what to do?"

"My mother kept a flock. I remember a few things. You can get baby chicks or pullets, that much I know. Pullets are easier—they're partly grown."

"Baby chicks. That's what I want."

Mama rolled her eyes. "How did I know that?"

I grinned at her.

"You don't have to have a rooster to have eggs, I remember that too. I think maybe roosters are a handful sometimes."

15

"But I want a rooster! I want to hear him crow." Our neighbor lady back home, Mrs. Perkins, had a big white rooster called Otis, and he crowed so loud, it was like he believed he was the one responsible for waking up the sun each day. In fact, he didn't just crow in the morning but whenever the mood struck him all day long.

Mama said, "Of course you do," and reached across the table to ruffle my hair.

"What else do you remember?"

"Not much, I'm afraid. It was my job to gather the eggs, and I didn't like to do it. I suppose my mother got tired of arguing with me, because after a while she just did it herself. You'll have to do a little research, I guess."

That afternoon we went to the library so I could read up on how to go about raising a flock of chickens. So far the library was about the only thing I really liked about Mama's hometown of New Paltz, New York. A library is a wonderful thing—all of our books combined couldn't hold a candle to the number of books a library has—and I'd never had one so close by before. Back home we had to drive thirty-eight miles of bad roads to go to one, and we didn't do that real often. Here it was only eight miles on pavement, and Mama was in the habit of taking me at least once a week. It was in a little old stone house on the main street that I purely loved—it made you just yearn to step in and start reading. I liked the librarian there too.

When I marched up to her desk and said I wanted to find

16

out everything I could about raising chickens, she nodded like that was not an out-of-the-way request at all. She asked if I knew how to use a computer, and when I said not too well, she nodded like that was nothing to get excited about either. I'd seen the computers at the library before, but I'd never tried them out. There was a computer at Mrs. Perkins's house back home, too, but it didn't work right. Those noisy little kids of hers had broken it about as soon as she dragged it home.

The librarian went ahead and showed me, and pretty soon I'd ventured out onto the Internet and read just about everything a person could read about chickens, plus some. I read and took notes and checked out three books she pulled aside for me, and by the time we left, I had a pretty good idea of what I wanted.

ME AND THE
AGWAY MAN

I was so excited that I begged Daddy to take me to the Agway in town the very next day. He had to go anyway, to get more paint for the birdhouses he makes to sell at the farmers' market, so he said okay.

I was all set with my order. I wanted twelve hens and one rooster. I would get three different kinds of hens: Silver-Laced Wyandottes and Australorps and Rhode Island Reds. I picked those breeds because I liked their names. Also because they were supposed to be good at getting along with one another and pretty generous with their eggs and not too faint of heart for the cold winters up north. I planned to order four of each. Also I would order a Leghorn rooster. I had seen a picture of one, and he looked just like Otis: snow white, with a big red comb.

It turned out things were not that easy. For one thing, I couldn't order just one rooster, or any rooster at all.

"You can't sell me just one Leghorn rooster?" I said to the man behind the counter at the Agway, giving him my most pleading look.

"No, I can't. It doesn't work that way. We don't sell roosters."

"Why not?" That seemed purely unbelievable to me.

"Most people don't want the bother of a rooster. They can be boisterous, and plus, they fertilize the eggs."

"What does that mean?"

The man looked pained and flung my daddy an alarmed look, but Daddy didn't say anything. The man cleared his throat. "Well, it means he plants a seed, like. To make a baby chicken. With the hen."

"Oh," I said, getting the picture.

"Most people don't want that. They just want hens for eggs. So the upshot is, we only sell female chicks—or we try to. It's hard to tell whether a chicken is a boy or a girl when it's a baby, so you *might* get a rooster in there. But you're not supposed to. The best way to get a rooster is to find someone who's giving one away. People are fickle, is what I've found. They think they want a rooster crowing in the morning but then they don't. They come back complaining he woke them up!"

I made a face. That was just silly, because crowing at dawn is the whole point of a rooster in the first place.

"They don't want the trouble of a big bold rooster strutting around, and maybe attacking 'em, too, if they haven't treated him right. You shouldn't have too much trouble finding one."

"But I wanted to raise him from when he's a baby!"

"Sorry," he said. He didn't sound sorry. I was surprised at how cranky he seemed, but probably he didn't have much fun, stuck behind that counter all day. I would've hated that—being indoors all the time, under the bright lights, breathing trapped-inside air. I was disappointed about the rooster, but I kept my chin up. "When can I get my chicks then?"

He checked a calendar he had on the counter. "It'll be a month for the Reds, a little more than that for the others."

"A whole *month*?"

"For good things, you have to wait. Welcome to farming, young lady."

I sighed, but I made my nod businesslike. "Okay then. That's what I want. Four of each of those kinds of chicks."

"There's a minimum order of six per breed."

"Six! I only want four of each, so I have twelve total."

"Six per pickup," he repeated. "That's the rule. And besides, pretty often some of the chicks don't survive. You should get a few extra anyway."

That gave me a sinking feeling but I nodded again, determined to be professional. I could hear Grammy's voice quoting one of her favorite sayings in my head like she was whispering in my ear: *It's a bad plan that can't be changed.* I said, "Okay then. I'll take six of each, please."

NO QUITTER

I wanted those chickens something fierce, for Grammy's leaving had put a big hole in my world. Finally, one morning in April, someone at the Agway called to say the first batch of chicks were in. I started hopping up and down in the middle of the living room floor. "Can we go and get them, Daddy?"

"This very minute?"

"Yes! They're *babies*. They need to come home right away."

Daddy had just put on his big rubber boots to

go out and begin tilling the garden, but after he leveled a kind of exasperated look at me, he sat back down and changed into his regular boots.

The same man as before was behind the counter. I told him my Rhode Island Reds were in and he led us over to a long table with cages full of chicks on them. I am not someone who normally gets real gushy, but they were *so darling*. They were just balls of fluff on little stick legs, and it was all I could do not to start jumping up and down again.

"So these are going to be your very own baby chickens, are they, missy?" he asked as we headed back to the register.

I didn't like his tone of voice much but I said, "Yes, sir, they are."

He gave me a smile I didn't think was really friendly. "I suppose you think they'll be like a pet."

"No, sir," I said, though I did think that in a way. "I'm going to sell the eggs."

He hooted. "You'll never make any money off of these few."

"I've got twelve more coming," I reminded him. "Silver-Laced Wyandottes and Australorps."

"Well, if you really wanted top-notch layers, you should've gotten Golden Comets."

I hadn't run across the name Golden Comets in my research or I might have ordered some—it did sound pretty. But all I said was "I ordered what I wanted." I didn't see that I had to be overly friendly, as he'd hardly been that to me. Daddy was frowning—he was getting fed up with the man. But he's not much of a talker, especially not with a stranger, and he didn't say anything.

The man added up my total and I handed over the money my folks loaned me to get started.

"Well," he said. "Just so you know, they're not going to stay cute like this. They're going to grow up, and I'll bet a dollar you lose interest in them then. Kids always do."

Daddy spoke up then. He looked at the man real flatlike and said, "You might be surprised, mister. My girl is no quitter. She knows her mind."

The man gave a disbelieving laugh that Daddy didn't hear. He'd already headed out the door to put the chicks in the truck. I didn't tell him about it. I was too busy feeling good about how he had stuck up for me.

THE
MISS NEW PALTZ

The rest of my chicks were in three days later. "They weren't scheduled to come until next week, but they're here," the man on the phone said. "Sorry about the change of plans."

"That's okay," I told him kindly. As soon as I hung up the phone, I whirled around to Mama, who was washing the dishes. "Mama, the rest of the chicks are in! Can we go and get them?"

"Well—in a little bit."

"Mama!"

"Prairie! How about helping me with these dishes and we'll get gone sooner."

I sighed, then went and grabbed a dishcloth.

When we got to town, Mama thought of all kinds of errands to run, and I was beside myself with impatience. I guess my fidgets got to Mama, because just as she was about to head into the grocery store parking lot, she flipped her blinker the other way and pulled into the diner across the street instead.

"I always loved this place," she said. "It's been here forever. How about you get a malt while I shop? Then we'll get the chicks, I promise."

The diner was big and silver, and it was called the Miss New Paltz. As soon as I went in, I decided it was the second thing I liked about New Paltz, New York. It had fat red booths to sit in and red stools on silver pedestals up at a long counter. The waitresses wore pale yellow dresses, the color of a store-bought egg yolk, and had name badges pinned to their chests.

The booth nearest the counter was filled with ladies drinking coffee. I looked them over once but didn't give any thought to them. I climbed onto a stool and ordered a chocolate malted with extra malt from the waitress, whose name tag said LOLLY. I thought that was a funny kind of a name to drag through life. Then I thought maybe that's why she was a nice, friendly waitress who didn't talk at a person like she was a baby, and didn't make a fuss over her accent either. Probably she got called "Lollipop" as a child and knew what it was like to be a fish out of water.

While I waited, I couldn't help overhearing what the women in the booth were saying. I had my back to them, so I suppose they didn't notice me.

One of them said, "Loren Lynn Patton is back living here now, you know, has been since last fall, though you hardly see hide nor hair of them. She came with that southern husband of hers, I don't know his name, and their little girl. Tom told me they were in the store the other day picking up baby chicks for the girl. If that isn't a waste of money, I don't know what is. They can't have two cents to rub together. Tom gets so tired of the way children always take on these projects and then lose interest."

I had sat up real straight at the mention of my mama's name, and I sat up even straighter at the mention of my poultry. I thought it was no wonder that the Agway man had seemed so crabby, with this mean lady waiting at home for him.

The lady went on. "It's silly for a child to raise chickens. Loren is just foolish for encouraging her. But that's the way she always was. No common sense. They'll never get anywhere trying to run her folks' farm, which is what I hear they're doing. Going to try and live off the land or some such nonsense. She's nothing but a dreamer."

"Now, Anne. You know Loren was always very creative," a soft voice said.

"Oh for pity's sake, Erma. She named that girl of hers Meadow."

29

A new voice said, "It's a wonder the county hasn't gone after them to get the girl put in school."

"She probably can't even read," the mean one named Anne answered.

I wanted to spin around on my stool and tell her, "My mama has plenty of common sense, if it's any of your business, which it isn't, and my daddy's name is Walton Evers. And I can so read, probably better than you. My grammy taught me at home and she did a good job of it. She was a schoolteacher back on Peabody Mountain in the little school they had before they built the big new one way off in town. Her mama before her taught in that same school, and we even have the big old dictionaries she used in her classroom. And my name is *Prairie*, not Meadow. There's a big difference. If you looked it up, you'd know."

I didn't do it, though. I wanted to keep listening.

"What can you expect with that kind of people," someone said. "Dirt-poor hillbillies."

"Fiddlesticks. Loren Lynn grew up right here, and I'm sure her husband is as nice as can be," the woman named Erma said, sounding vexed despite her gentle way of speaking.

"Well, I don't see what—" the one named Anne began and then stopped short. I looked over my shoulder, and there was Mama coming in. Guilty, I thought, flashing them a look. Guilty, guilty, guilty. I thought that of all except the soft-voiced one—Erma—but she should've chosen her friends better. I marched past them without another glance as we went out the

30

door. I would not deign to give them one speck of notice. I was sure that was what Grammy would advise. I didn't tell Mama about them either. I didn't want to make her sad.

The fact is that those ladies were wrong about everything they said. Grammy taught me more than most kids learn going to regular school (which I know because the neighbor kids on Peabody Mountain were always behind me in their studies *and* they had to ride the bus an hour to school each day, which as Grammy said was a pure waste of time for a young person). Mama and Daddy carried on with my schooling right where she left off, and while maybe they didn't have quite her knack of making every last thing in the world interesting, they did not slack off in keeping my studies going.

They were right to help get me started in the chicken business too. How many of those ladies had a flock of good laying hens, plus maybe even a handsome rooster, like I was going to? I'd bet zero.

7

RAISING BABIES

Raising babies wasn't as easy as I'd expected. Being in charge of six chicks was alarming enough, but once I had all eighteen of them in the brooder we found in the barn—a brooder is just a box with a lightbulb in it to keep the chicks warm—things got really hectic. For one thing, I couldn't tell the Australorps from the Wyandottes. They all looked the same—black and white—and none of them looked quite like their pictures. Besides that, they were all so busy toddling about and cheeping that I didn't have a prayer of keeping them straight anyway.

Even that first night, when I only had the Reds, I could hardly sleep. Were they too warm or too cold? Had they gotten enough to eat? Had they somehow blundered into their water dish and spilled it all over? They'd catch their deaths of damp and cold if that was so. I kept leaping up to check on them, and one time I was convinced they were dead, every last one. I went running for Mama and Daddy, but it turned out they were fine—just sleeping splayed out in deathlike poses.

"You all have broken my heart into smithereens already," I told them sternly, but they didn't seem to be listening.

Another thing I discovered is that chickens poop a lot, a truth that my research had not prepared me for. It takes a considerable amount of changing to keep their bedding clean, or even cleanish. Daddy said chickens produced the best fertilizer you could hope for and he'd get good use out of it in the gardens, but that didn't make me like it any better.

Also, the chicks were rambunctious in a way that no amount of reading could have shown me. They bullied and fought, and I admit it alarmed me. I didn't know when I should step in and when I should let them work things out themselves. I wasn't sure if they were playing or if they were really going to hurt each other, especially since the Reds were a tiny bit bigger and stronger than the others, being just that little bit older.

I wrote to Grammy telling her my worries—we were always writing letters back and forth because Great-Uncle Tecumseh didn't have a phone—and she wrote back and said I had to do the best I could and hope it worked out. Her advice sounded calm, but it was not so easy. Every time I turned around, there was some new cause for worry, and once in a while I wondered what I'd gotten myself into.

It was sad sometimes, too, for it was true what the man at the Agway said. The chicks didn't all live. One of the Reds died on the fourth day I had them, and a week later, right when I was thinking everything was fine, one of the others died. I cried quite a lot over both, and Daddy and Mama and I held a ceremony for their burials out in the yard. Daddy let me use his paints to inscribe a big rock with the names I gave them after they'd passed: Willow and Fleece. I still couldn't tell the chicks apart, really, but I didn't want to lay them to rest nameless.

I went to the Agway with Daddy when he needed some garden seeds a few days after Fleece passed away, and the man named Tom was behind the counter again.

"The budding poultry woman." He sounded friendlier than before. "My wife told me you're Loren Patton's daughter. Your grandmother always raised a nice flock of hens. I used to buy eggs from her. How are your chicks?"

"They're fine. Mostly." Then I blurted out, "Two of them died. I did my best to coddle them and build them up, I gave them supplements and everything. I made sure they had enough to eat and drink and kept them warm. I don't know what I did wrong."

"The weaker chicks usually don't survive no matter what you do," he said, quite kindly. "It's not your fault. It's the way of the world, is what it is."

And life did go on, for what else can it do?

The chicks that were left were as lively as anything, and by the end of the second week I was worrying less. I was beginning to have my favorites too. There was Bootstrap, who was a Rhode Island Red brave enough to sit on my lap, and Ezekiel, who was so big and bossy, I really hoped he might be a rooster. Also I decided that two chicks I named Miss Emily and Miss Polly were sisters. They were so alike—delicate in their manners and shy. I was pretty sure they were Silver-Laced Wyandottes, mostly because it was such a pretty name, just right for such ladies.

All in all the chicks kept me so busy that I didn't have much time to feel lonesome. That was a good thing, because with the advent of spring, Mama and Daddy were busier than ever with their projects and chores.

Back in North Carolina, Daddy had a job at a furniture factory and only made his birdhouses as a sideline. But now Mama and Daddy wanted to make their living from the farm and from their crafts, with no outside job at all, and even I could see that was going to take a lot of doing. Between reclaiming the berry patch, and tilling and planting and tending the gardens and flower beds, and Daddy making a whole stockpile of birdhouses, and Mama sewing up quilts as if her life depended upon it, they were busy every minute. They were so tired at night that pretty often Daddy fell asleep in the recliner and Mama had to jostle him awake to make him go off to bed. One night I wrote and told Grammy I wasn't the only one who missed her. I said I was sure Mama and Daddy wished just as hard as I did that she'd come up north and live with us again, and help with everything like she used to. I said we needed her way more than Great-Uncle Tecumseh ever could.

In her next letter Grammy didn't answer that exactly. She only said that Great-Uncle Tecumseh had wrenched his knee and couldn't crawl around in the garden putting his seeds in like usual. She said she was doing it for him but was about ready to string him up by his shirt collar, he was so cantankerous about every last thing.

LOVE

In June, Mama and Daddy and I started going to the farmers' markets that were held all around. There was one in Kingston on Saturdays, and Woodstock on Wednesdays, and one right in New Paltz on Sundays. We'd get up early in the morning and load everything we had to sell—just the birdhouses and quilts at first, then the garden vegetables and berries as they came on—into the back of the pickup and cover it with a big tarp. Then Daddy would ease out of the driveway and go real slow along the back roads to whichever town we were headed for that day. He would never get on Interstate 87. There was too much traffic there, he said, and he was afraid the truck might have heart failure at the speed of it. Also he didn't want to call any undue attention to the fact that the muffler was more or less shot and he hadn't gotten around to getting a New York State inspection sticker just yet.

I liked those times. The radio would be set to the oldies station, playing rock-and-roll songs from when Mama and Daddy were young. Mama would be sipping her coffee from a ceramic mug she made once, and Daddy would be smoking a cigarette with his window cracked open to let the smoke trail out. I nagged and nagged at him to quit, but that was his morning coffee, he said, and I couldn't expect a man to venture out into the world without his coffee, could I? I'd sit in between them feeling snug and a little sleepy, wondering what the day would bring, singing along if a song came on that I liked.

We did that all spring and summer. We sold berries and flowers and vegetables, and Mama's quilts and Daddy's birdhouses. He builds them out of scrap wood and paints them in soft, rainy-looking colors with pictures of vines and flowers twining around. If I were a bird, I know I would want to fly right in. People like them too. They sell at a brisk pace, and folks are always smiling when they carry one away. I think it's because of all the love Daddy puts in while he's making them. People can just feel it, even if they don't know what it is they are feeling.

It's the same way with the quilts. Mama loves to make them. Not me. I help out some, but sewing cannot hold my interest long. Making a blanket is like climbing a mountain with a million small steps. It is one tiny stitch after another, stitch after stitch, never ending. I always ask her, "Why not just sew two big chunks of cloth together, a back and a front, and call it done?"

Mama laughs when I say that. She shakes her head and says, "Prairie Evers. The fun is in putting the colors and shapes together."

"That's crazy," I always say back to tease her, but the truth is I love Mama's blankets. She picks out the prettiest hues, things you wouldn't guess would go together, but then they do.

I watched her one hot August night as she sat at the sewing machine, turning a block this way and that. She was making a starburst pattern, and every stitch and piece had to be just so or it would never come out right in the end. She had been at it for hours, and I could tell by the way she shifted in her seat and shrugged her shoulders every little while that she was weary. I went and leaned against her work table. "Don't you ever get tired of it, Mama?"

"Tired of what?"

I ran a finger down the edge of a seam in the little pile of finished squares she had stacked up. "This."

She sighed. "Well, I'm worn out tonight, I won't deny it. But no, I don't ever seem to get tired of making quilts. It's a foolish thing, I guess, stitching little pieces of fabric together, but

I love it. I have these patterns in my head, and I have to make them come out into the world somehow." She wrinkled her nose and smiled.

I watched for a while longer and then wandered outside to find Daddy. He was in the vegetable garden, pulling hornworms from the tomato plants. The hornworms were fat and green and blended in with the stalks. Daddy peered at each plant, put every worm he found in an old coffee can, and when he was sure a plant was clean, crawled on to the next. After a while I said, "Daddy, do you get tired?"

"What's that, chicklet?"

"Do you get tired of doing stuff like this all the time? Pulling caterpillars off the tomatoes and making a ton of birdhouses that are kind of all the same and pulling weeds that just grow back overnight."

He sat back on his heels and squinted at me. "Well. It needs doing."

I kept watching him. I was not satisfied with his answer. After a little bit he looked up again. He scratched the back of his head. "You want to help?"

I shrugged and crouched down on the opposite side of the plant he was working on. The evening sun felt like a warm cloth on my neck. I squinted at the tomato plant, breathing real soft. Bootstrap wandered up the garden row and pecked in the dirt behind me. I smelled warm earth and green vineyness and almost-ripe tomatoes. I saw a hornworm, his antennae waving.

I reached out and pulled him off the vine, then dropped him in Daddy's can. We worked our way down the row this way and then up the next one. "You ever feel like getting out of the chicken business?" Daddy asked about midway along.

I glanced at him real sharp to see what he meant, but he was looking at the tomato. "No," I said.

"Do you love every minute of it all the time?"

I thought about cleaning up after them. "No."

A little smile twitched around his lips. "Well, there you go then."

When we were done, Daddy gave me the can of hornworms to feed to the chickens. Those poor caterpillars (for that's what they are, not worms really; Daddy and I looked it up in one of his garden books) were devoured in about two skinny minutes, but the chickens were as happy as anything.

THE EGG

A few days later when I went to the hen-house to clean the nest boxes, there in the straw was an egg. An *egg*. It wasn't much bigger than a big marble, but it was perfect: egg shaped and smooth and brown. "An egg!" I whispered. I reached out to touch it, and it was still warm. I cupped it in my hand and ran outside.

"Whose is this?" I demanded—the hens were ambling around pecking at the ground beneath the maple tree—but of course they didn't answer. I suddenly realized there might be more—there might be a lot!—so I ran back in and looked in the other boxes, but they were empty. Next I headed for the vegetable patch where Mama and Daddy were working. When I got there, I just held my palm out. The egg wobbled there shyly. I was so proud, I couldn't even speak.

Mama made a ceremony of frying it up for my lunch, though I debated at first whether to eat it. It was so tiny and sweet. But what else was there to do? It was an egg, not a piece of china. I had it fried easy and smashed on a half slice of toast.

The next day I found three eggs. The day after that I found none. But the next day there were four and then three after that, and by the end of the week I had my first dozen.

10

BYE-BYE, MISS AMERICAN PIE

That next Wednesday started out like any other, except it was going to be the first time I tried to sell my eggs. We got up early and loaded the truck and headed for Woodstock. A song I liked came on the radio and I started singing along. I just knew my twelve eggs were going to sell, and this was only the beginning. In another week, I might have a dozen more. "Bye-bye, Miss American Pie," I sang. "Drove my Chevy to the levee but the levee was dry—"

I especially liked that tune because it had a Chevy in it, and that's what we drove, a Chevy. I stopped singing long enough to say, "Daddy?"

Daddy said, "Hmm?"

"What's a levee?"

"Oh, it's a kind of embankment."

"What's it for?"

"Well, to hold water back, I guess. Usually."

"Why would a guy drive a Chevy there?"

"Well, now. I don't know. Could be all sorts of reasons, I suppose."

Daddy looked thoughtful, like he was thinking over the reasons a guy might drive a Chevy to a levee. He took a drag on his cigarette and then let the tip hang out the window again. I poked his leg, hard, which was my signal to him that he should not be smoking, and he patted my leg back real gentle to say, *I know, little chicklet, and someday maybe I'll quit, but not right now.* I had to be satisfied with that, and he had to put up with my nagging. After a while he said, "You know, I don't really know that I do know exactly what a levee is, now that you mention it. I guess we'll have to look it up when we get home."

"Oh," I said. "Okay." By then the chorus had come around the second time. I set into singing again, belting it out pretty good. Before long Mama joined in, and even Daddy sang a line here and there. We pulled into the parking lot at the farmers' market sounding like a rock concert. The man getting out of the vehicle next to ours gave us a look, and I thought, Well, you just don't know how to have fun, mister.

I felt purely happy at that moment. Except for the fact that Grammy wasn't there, life was perfect. It was still summer, and I loved summer. Pretty soon it would be fall, and I loved fall too. My hens were laying, the gardens were growing, Mama and Daddy were tired but happy, and Daddy had promised that the minute he got a spare second he was going to put a platform up in the fork of the maple tree for me so I would have a tree house. Lately I was starting to think Ezekiel wasn't a rooster after all, and wondering if an Australorp I'd named Fiddle just might be. He—or she—had been getting bigger and bossier by the minute, and every day I waited for a crow that would prove my suspicion. All in all I thought it'd be hard to improve on things, if you weren't going to move back to North Carolina, which I knew we weren't. I sighed with contentment and scrambled after Mama out the passenger-side door.

What I thought later about that day is how you never know when something big is headed straight at you. One day Grammy and I were playing Monopoly, and the next day she was on a bus going back to Vine's Cove. One day I was snug and happy in between my folks on our way to the market, and the next— Well, you just never know.

THE BEST OF
TIMES AND THE
WORST OF TIMES

There was a story written a long time ago that
Grammy liked to quote from: "It was the best of
times, it was the worst of times" is how it began. I
never understood that. How could something be
two opposite ways at once? But it's true, it can be.

Midway through that Wednesday at the market
a lady came up to our booth and said to her friend,
"Jennifer, I haven't seen a quilt like this since I was
down in Kentucky. Would you look at this. Would

you look at this pattern. And the colors. It's so bold. Very unique."

Her friend agreed, and the lady asked my mama, "How much is it?"

Mama was about to tell her two hundred and fifty dollars. That's what we always charged. But something got into me. I said to myself, The clothes that woman is wearing probably cost that much. I'll bet she wouldn't bat an eyelash at paying more. It wouldn't hurt to ask. I stepped up and said, "Five hundred dollars." Mama looked at me like I had taken leave of my senses.

The lady said, "I just think I have to take it. What do you think, Jennifer?"

Jennifer had a cell phone up to her ear and she was talking about shallots and lamb chops to someone, and should she get a bottle of Bordeaux for dinner, but she stopped long enough to say, "It's beautiful; I think five hundred is a good price."

"Yes, I think so too," the lady said, rolling her eyes at Jennifer, who didn't notice. She winked at me and made a little snapping motion with her hand that said, *Talk, talk, talk*. I couldn't help but grin. A minute later that lady took Mama's quilt away with her after writing a check for five hundred dollars with no more fuss than if it had been for five. She bought my eggs too. My very first sale, from my very own flock of hens. I wanted to hop up and down, but I didn't.

The lady pulled a crisp five-dollar bill out of her wallet and told me to keep the change. I was going to put the dollar tip in our cash box, but Mama said no. She was laughing. "Act like a kid and not a little old banker lady, why don't you? Just for a minute? You put that in your pocket. I guess you've paid off the debt on the chickens plus some, you brought in so much extra on that quilt."

I didn't like to do that, I wanted to figure it out exact, as I intended to pay back all it took to get me started in egg farming. But Mama said, "Don't worry. We'll figure it out once we get home, if you must. Wait until I tell your dad." Daddy was off a few stands away, visiting with a man who made honey.

So I shoved that five-dollar bill in my pocket and was about to go looking around. That's what I do sometimes, if we aren't too busy. Mama and Daddy don't mind, as long as I check in every little while.

But just then a woman came up to us. It gave me a start, because she was the meanest coffee-drinking lady from the Miss New Paltz Diner. I recognized her pinched-up face. She said, "Oh, such a sweet little girl, did she help with all this work?"

Mama studied the woman pretty careful without answering.

"I'm surprised to see a child here when school's just started today."

Mama said, "Is there something I can help you with?"

The lady picked up a birdhouse and turned it every which way, oohing and aahing and making out that she was nice and friendly, but of course I knew better. Daddy came back just then, and the lady started in on him. Wasn't it a fine day, and wasn't this a gorgeous birdhouse, it must've taken some work to make it, and who did all this work? Did his little girl do it, and shouldn't she be in school?

Daddy took the birdhouse from her, kind of gentle but firm, and set it back down on the display table. He said, "Were you wanting to buy something, ma'am?"

The lady looked at Daddy real sharp. "Your daughter *does* go to school?"

Mama and Daddy glanced at each other. "We teach her at home," Daddy said.

"Oh, I see." The lady sized me up like a hawk hovering atop a mouse. "I'll bet you want to go to school, though, don't you, sweetheart?"

"What for?"

She laughed. "Why, to be educated and learn your basics."

"I learned my basics a long time ago."

The look on her face said she didn't think so. "You've got a computer and books and all the other things the kids have at school so they'll know what's what out in the world?"

I frowned at her. "I have about a million books, and my mama and daddy have a million more. And I know how to use a computer." I was glad I had been to the library and researched my chickens that way. "I know just about everything there is to know about one. Besides which, some things are not all they're cracked up to be."

"Well, *well*. Aren't you the smart one? Don't you want to go to school to be with children your own age?"

"I don't like children much." I didn't know as I exactly meant that—I didn't really know very many kids—but I thought it might make her go away.

"Is that so?" She raised her eyebrows. "And tell me, what will you be when you grow up?"

"I'll go on raising my hens and selling the eggs, and do like we've always done."

"Oh goodness," she said, sounding very amused.

I looked at her real steady.

She laughed, and not in a nice way.

That made me mad. "You have not been raised correctly if you don't know any better than to laugh at a person. And the way you pull your hair back tight from your face makes your nose look even longer than it is. You ought to think about changing it."

Mama said, "Prairie."

Before Mama could say anything else, I told the lady, "I beg your pardon, ma'am," but I didn't mean it. I wanted to tell her, "You're as plain as a water spigot and mean as rain in January," and I only kept quiet out of consideration for Mama's feelings.

The lady gave us all a disgusted look. "I can see you don't remember me, Loren Lynn. I did think about buying one of these birdhouses as a gift for my son, he just got a nice promotion at the bank, but I'm afraid they are just overpriced. And I must say, it's a shame a child of this age is not in school, learning to be among other children and learning some manners, too. Obviously she doesn't know a thing about that if she'll speak to an adult like she just spoke to me. Mark my words, you'll be sorry someday."

"Who was that?" Daddy asked after she stalked away.

"That has to be Anne Oliver. I haven't seen her in fifteen years."

"She don't seem real fond of you." A grin quirked at the corner of Daddy's mouth.

Mama looked upset. "She's not, she never was. I beat her son in a spelling bee way back in the fifth grade, and I swear it started then. Plus, my mother always got the top prize for canning at the county fair and my dad was elected over her husband as township clerk three years running."

Daddy rolled his eyes, and Mama shook her head. "Some people just don't have enough to keep them occupied, I guess."

The next moment, the lady who bought the quilt came back.

She said to my mama, "I have an idea I'm just too excited to keep to myself. You tell me what you think of it, and if you say no, I'll understand. But your work is so good. Your use of color, and the patterns— Well, I'm not telling you anything you don't know. But I direct a community arts program in New Paltz, and I just wondered if there's a chance you'd consider giving some classes this fall. There's a hole in the curriculum and the minute I bought this quilt I knew just how to fill it."

Mama's eyes had gone wide. "You're kidding."

"I most certainly am not!" The lady had one of those smiles that you couldn't help grinning back at.

"We live in New Paltz!" Mama exclaimed.

"Well, that will work out beautifully, then."

I was so proud for my mama right then. I didn't give any thought to what it might mean to me.

BETRAYAL

The next morning I rolled out of bed and went to my window. It was sunny and mild and I had the blossoming feeling I get when a day seems full of promise. In the night I'd heard coyotes wailing. It seemed like a good omen, even though I knew I'd have to be extra careful about my chickens and never fail to put them back in the coop at night, or else they'd get eaten. I always loved to hear the coyotes howl back on Peabody Mountain. They sounded so wild and free and mysterious.

Hearing them here, too, made it seem like there was a thread strung out between me and Grammy.

I gazed out at the gardens and barn and chicken coop, the pointy-topped hemlock and the meadow rolling down toward town. Maybe today I'd try to coax our new cats out from the shadows in the barn. Yesterday Daddy had gotten two—one gray and one black—from a man at the farmers' market. Daddy wanted them to keep the mice down, but I wanted them just for themselves. So far I'd hardly caught sight of them, but Mama said if I was patient they'd lose their shyness.

But that would be later. First I had to let the chickens out and clean the nest boxes. Then maybe I'd walk to the woods. I could make it a nature walk, which Grammy and I did pretty often as part of my schooling. There was a little twisty-armed shrub along the lane. If I took a tree guide, maybe I could learn its name. I could draw a picture of it and write a poem, too. Mama had me doing haiku lately.

Small twisty-armed shrub would do for the first line, I thought as I rifled through my bureau drawer, looking for my favorite shirt. I'd worn it so much, it was soft and thin and had a hole under the arm, but I wouldn't let Mama get rid of it. *Along the lane to the woods. What name do you use?*

I found my shirt and pulled it on, still planning. Maybe I'd take my BB gun. It was my daddy's when he was a boy, and pretty often I did target practice on a bale of straw he set up for me in the pasture. I liked to take aim and hit the bull's-eye.

You never know when a skill like that could come in handy—if a coyote went after my chickens, for example, though I don't know how I'd ever have the heart to pull the trigger. For my chickens, I guess I'd have to. Mostly I liked to pretend I was a girl from olden times, living in a cabin with her folks and her grandma. Pretty often I added a sister or an orphan we'd adopted into the story too. I'd pretend a band of robbers had come to the door, and there I was, ready to defend us.

I thought I'd pack a lunch too. After lunch, I'd do my inside lessons—math and composition today—and write to Grammy. I'd tell her about selling my eggs, and the class Mama was going to teach, and the coyotes. I'd remind her of the story she always told me when we went outside to see the stars at night, of how Coyote led four wolves into the sky and left them there to make the Big Dipper. She'd like that I remembered.

I hurried downstairs to get started.

Mama had fixed oatmeal for breakfast, which is not my favorite, even with maple syrup on it. I got through it by eating as quick as I could, and was set to take my bowl to the sink and head to the henhouse when Daddy said, "Hold on a minute, chicklet."

Something in his tone of voice alerted me. "What?" I said, feeling wary.

"Your mama and I have something to talk over with you."

That didn't sound like good news. They didn't have anything to talk over either. "Talk over" sounds like you can put your two cents in, but instead they had something to tell me. They had decided I should go to school.

You could have knocked me over with the smallest, downiest chicken feather. I could not imagine a worse idea. Mrs. Perkins's kids back home went to school and they'd told me plenty about it. In school you were trapped inside all day, and you had to sit still in a chair, and you had to learn by memorizing textbooks instead of reading all the interesting books Grammy used with me. There'd be no more wandering the fields and the woods whenever I wanted, no more going to the farmers' markets except on the weekend, no more checking for eggs at noon as well as in the morning and at night. The shape of my days would be ruined. And the kids would be like the Perkins kids—rowdy and wearing. Worse than that, they'd be mean. I had read plenty of books and I knew. Kids don't like kids who are different. I was from North Carolina and had never attended school, just for starters. What were my folks thinking? It was going to be a disaster.

"We don't live on Peabody Mountain anymore," Daddy was saying. "This school is just eight miles away, not thirty-eight on a bad road."

"You'll make friends. You won't be so lonely. And there's more to learn than we can teach you now," Mama said.

"I already know plenty and I'm not lonely." It didn't seem like she heard me. "I'm not lonely," I said louder.

"There are all kinds of things to do at school. They even have a swimming pool."

"I hate to swim!" That was a flat-out lie. Mama reached out to smooth my hair, but I yanked myself away. "All you care about is your new job at the Arts Center! If Grammy were here, she'd put a stop to this. Grammy always taught me good."

"Taught you *well*," Mama corrected gently, but I ignored her. I whipped around to look at Daddy beseechingly.

"Your grammy always did a real fine job," Daddy said. "But she thinks the same as us. We talked about it some before she left."

"You did not," I yelled. But Mama and Daddy looked at me so kindly, I knew they had.

"We shouldn't have put this off," Daddy said to Mama. And Mama said, "No," looking sorrowful and shaking her head.

"Stop talking about me like I'm not here! You're just afraid of that lady, Anne Oliver. You're afraid she's going to cause trouble for you."

Mama sighed. "I'm not afraid of Anne Oliver, chicklet. But I have to admit she got me thinking even harder than I was before. Sometimes it's hard to hear the truth, hardest coming from someone you don't like. The fact is that your daddy and I decided when we moved up here that you should go to school this fall. We talked it over with Grammy. She thought the change would be good. She was worried you were spending all your time just with old folks. We all decided that this would be best."

"*No!* That's wrong. Everything was *fine* the way it was."

Mama went on like I hadn't spoken. "But then I—well, I put it off. I thought, one more year— I knew how I was going to miss having you around home all the time. But that was wrong of me."

"No it wasn't! It was right. You were right. I should stay home."

Mama reached out to smooth my hair again. "We really do think it's a good idea for you to go to school now that we don't live so far from town. For one thing, your daddy and I just don't have the time we should to devote to your studies with all this work on the farm."

"We can all stay up later!"

Mama's smile said that wasn't going to happen. "And besides that, you're old enough now that going to school is important. It'd be good to have friends your own age. There's nothing else like it. Don't you miss the Perkins kids?"

"No!" I didn't either.

"Wouldn't you like to have a girlfriend, a best friend?"

"No." I'd make sure not to mention the imaginary sister I'd invent on my jaunts around the woods.

"And there's so much to learn—"

"I don't care about learning."

"Oh, you do so."

I scowled with my whole entire self.

"I went to that school, you know. I had a pretty good time there. If you go to the library, you could find my pictures in the old yearbooks. Wouldn't you like to see your mama when she was young and funny looking?"

The thought of going to the same school as Mama did tickle my interest some, but I wasn't going to show it. "I won't learn anything in school, and you can't make me."

Mama gave me a look over the tops of her spectacles. "Well, I'm sorry if you don't like the idea, but I'm afraid that's the way it's going to be. We've already decided."

I felt so betrayed that I started crying, which made me madder than ever.

SCHOOL

It all happened fast. Mama and Daddy took me to the school office on Friday and got everything set up. Before I knew it I was enrolled, and the principal smiled at me and told me he was glad I would be one of his students. The smile I gave back to him was so-so at best.

Mama took me shopping for clothes and things Friday night. By the end of the evening I owned two new pairs of blue jeans and some bright white tennis shoes and three new shirts and a cherry-red sweater with white trim at the cuffs and collar. I knew all that took a big bite out of Mama and Daddy's budget and I knew it was nice of them, but even so, it was hard for me to really like any of it, even the red sweater, because it was all for the purpose of going to school.

I didn't want to go to school for a thousand reasons, one of which was that it was going to be so hard to be away from my chickens. There was too much happening. On Sunday, Fiddle had looked at me and crowed, a half strangled *erk-erk-err-err*.

I ran to where Daddy was working in the barn and told him, "Daddy, I was right, Fiddle is a rooster! He just crowed! He really did!"

Daddy grinned at me. "Isn't that something."

"It is! It's amazing! Daddy, I *can't* go to school now."

His look turned skeptical. "And why is that?"

"Well, because. Because Fiddle's a rooster, and he's crowing, and he's going to get better at it, and if I'm at school, I won't be here to hear it."

"Uh-huh," Daddy said.

"Please, Daddy. Please say I don't have to go."

I clasped my hands in front of me and put all the pleading in my soul into my eyes, but Daddy had only squeezed my shoulder and said, "You have to go, chicklet. Might as well get used to it."

But even up to the last minute, I still hoped I could somehow put a stop to school. On Monday morning I told Mama I was not going.

"No," I told her. "No, no, no." I flung myself out the door and ran to the henhouse. I climbed in and shut the door behind me.

Mama let me go for a spell, and then she came looking. "Prairie! It's about time to catch the bus. Come get your breakfast."

I sat real still, but the hens gave me away. They were flustered at being shut in with me and had begun to cluck and fuss. I couldn't blame them. A chicken is a chicken, after all. Mama opened the door. We gazed at each other.

"It really won't be so awful."

"It will so. I've read enough to know. The teachers'll be mean and the kids'll be worse and I won't have any friends and they'll all make fun of me."

"Chicklet, it won't be that bad. You might even like it."

"I will not."

"Well," Mama said with a sigh. "Maybe not. But nonetheless you are going."

Finally I came out and stood before her, scowling. But Mama gave me such a kindly look, I nearly started to bawl. She pulled a piece of straw from my hair. "Dust yourself off and come eat. I'll fry you some eggs."

DAY ONE

From day one I did not like school. First of all I didn't like the big yellow bus roaring up to fetch me. I could hear it coming from a half mile off, and I worried the noise would upset the hens out of laying, especially Miss Emily and Miss Polly, who were so shy.

I didn't like being in among all those kids. Every one of them stared at me when I climbed on board the bus, and not with a kind look either. I wasn't much used to children and I didn't believe I'd like them, just like I told Anne Oliver. One here and there might be all right, but not a whole flock bunched up together. Right away I could tell it would be just like in the henhouse: there was going to be a pecking order, and I was going to be at the bottom of it.

The bus was bad, but school was worse. There were more kids in that building than I ever saw in one place before, and they were going every which way, yelling at the tops of their voices. I dreaded being caged among them all day. It was like the Perkins kids back home times a thousand.

I didn't like the bright lights shining down on my head. I didn't like the smell of the place. I didn't like the bells clanging. Most of all I didn't like the way people constantly stared at me, like my pants were ripped, which they weren't. I was wearing a pair of those new blue jeans and a new shirt and the new shoes too, and it felt like the corners of all those new things were poking at me.

That first morning, I went to the room the principal had showed us when I was getting enrolled, which was the fifth-grade classroom, the grade I would be in just as if I'd gone to school right along. I stuck my hand out to the lady teacher who was standing at the door. She looked surprised but she took my hand and gave it a good firm shake.

"You must be Prairie Evers," she said.

"Yes, ma'am."

"My name is Mrs. Hanson."

"Yes, ma'am."

"So you can call me that."

"Yes, ma'am."

She smiled, but not in a mean way. "Now, we have a few rules you'll have to follow here. You can't bring video games or your cell phone into the classroom with you. You have to leave them in your locker. All right?"

"Yes, ma'am," I said.

"Do you have anything you want to go put back in your locker?"

"No, ma'am." I didn't think it was necessary to say I didn't own any of those things. My aunt Arla gave me a video game for Christmas one year, and it was fun for a little while, but then the batteries ran down and we didn't get to town right away to get more. By the time I got back to it, the Perkins's dog had got ahold of it and used it for a chew toy, and that was the end of that.

Mrs. Hanson studied me real close, as if to decide if I was telling the truth. She seemed to decide I was. "All right, then. You'll sit in the second row. We're set up by alphabetical order."

I said, "Yes, ma'am, Mrs. Hanson," and hiked up my sack lunch and my notebook and pencil box full of sharp new pencils, and went and sat in row two, three chairs back, where there was an empty desk waiting.

Not one of the kids in that room gave me a welcoming look. Some of them were making noises and laughing. I sat real still and looked straight ahead at the blackboard. I pretended to myself I was a coyote, watching from the edge of the woods, making sure it was safe to move before I did. A coyote is smart; you can do worse than to follow a coyote's way.

On the blackboard Mrs. Hanson had written "Please welcome Prairie Evers."

That explained why some of those kids were making whooshing noises. Probably they meant to be wind blowing through prairie grass. Others of them made chuffing noises and stomped their feet, to be buffalo I guess. Some were hooting; they meant to be wild Indians I imagine.

I am real dark. I have brown hair that is almost black, and brown eyes, and my skin turns brown in the sun faster than you can say spit. I'd been outside all summer, so I was about as brown as garden dirt. A coyote would not move a muscle in this situation, I thought to myself. A coyote would just bide his time. So that's what I did.

Mrs. Hanson said, "Class," real sharp. It surprised me. I wouldn't have thought she had such a sharp voice in her. It was like the slap of a leather strop against a table. "Class," she said again, and after a minute those kids quieted down.

One student didn't hoot and holler and make prairie noises. She sat in the next aisle over, three chairs back, just like me. She had long blond hair and wore a faded blue T-shirt that looked comfortable. She looked quiet. I tried giving her a little smile. She didn't smile back, but she didn't frown either.

Mrs. Hanson said, "Open your books to page twenty-three, please."

I looked over at the quiet girl to see what book Mrs. Hanson meant. The girl held up her book so I could see: it was the reading book. I pulled mine out and opened to page twenty-three.

NEW RULES

I'd never been as tired as I was after sitting in school all day that first week. I barely had the energy to check for eggs when I got home, and it was all I could do to go outside in the morning and set the hens and Fiddle free. I felt jealous every time I watched them amble out and start pecking the dirt for bugs and grubs like nothing was wrong.

Every day the bus roared up to fetch me and I trudged aboard. There was always room near the front to sit by myself, and that's what I did. At school I couldn't keep out of trouble. I thought I could get a drink of water or sharpen a pencil or go to the restroom whenever I needed, but that was wrong. Even after I knew the rules, it was hard to stay put. I felt like I'd crawl out of my skin, and I didn't see how the other kids could stand it. I guess they just had more practice than me at waiting for the different bells to ring. When we got let out for recess, they'd go tearing out of the building like ants streaming off a burning anthill.

I didn't hurry to get out for recess. There was nothing much to do. It wasn't like there were any woods I could go tromping around in, and it was just like I thought with the other kids. They all knew each other and didn't know me, and didn't want to.

At first some of the boys teased me. They'd call "Hey, Field!" and then break down laughing. I got it: hey, field—hayfield—prairie. Ha-ha. I didn't answer. I'd just lean against the fence in my sharp-edged new clothes, or sit on a swing and wait for the bell to ring. Before long they didn't even bother with teasing me.

It wasn't much better inside. I was used to the way Grammy did things. With her I always just blurted out whatever I wondered and whatever I knew, but it wasn't like that in school. Mrs. Hanson was always having to tell me to wait until I was called on, or to give someone else a turn. Pretty soon I just kept quiet. A lot of those kids didn't like that I had so much to say—they thought I was showing off.

On the playground one day a girl named Amabelle who sat

in my same row bumped into me real hard where I was leaning against the fence. "Hey," I told her. "Watch where you're going."

She had three other girls with her, and they were all glaring. "You think you're so smart," Amabelle said. "You better watch it."

I was scared for just a minute. I saw in their eyes that they wouldn't mind lighting into me. Then in the next second I was mad. I stood up straight and took a step toward them. "*You* better watch out."

I didn't know what I'd do next, but I didn't have to figure it out. One of them tugged on Amabelle's arm and said, "Somebody's coming," and they all turned and ran. I leaned back against the fence.

The quiet girl from the next row over had been watching. Her name was Ivy Blake, I now knew. When I looked at her, she quickly glanced away.

16

WEEK TWO

Monday morning of week two I came downstairs and told Mama I didn't feel good. "I think I have the flu."

She put the back of her hand up against my forehead. "You don't feel warm. Does your stomach hurt?"

I nodded. It did.

"Do you feel achy?"

"Yes." I felt achy and slow all over.

"You seemed quiet all weekend. Maybe you're coming down with something." She sighed. "Probably it's being around all those germs you're not used to."

I mashed oatmeal up against the side of my bowl with the back of my spoon. Then I pushed the bowl away. I could not imagine eating.

"Maybe you'd better stay home. I think I'll call the school."

I trudged up the stairs and got under the covers. Mama came and checked on me and asked if I wanted hot tea or ginger ale, but I told her no, "I just want to sleep." But I didn't want that either. I didn't know what I wanted. I lay in bed all morning. In the afternoon I got up and sat in the rocker by the potbelly stove. I tried to write Grammy a letter, but I couldn't think of anything to say, so I went outside and sat in the tire swing Daddy hung for me and watched the chickens for a while.

Fiddle was strutting about the yard like a king. He looked very handsome, with his curling tail and broad chest, his soft black feathers with their shiny green sheen. He carried himself so tidy and proud, like a little general, and that did make me smile. But even watching Fiddle didn't really make me feel better. It just reminded me of what I was missing every day while I was at school. After a while I wandered to the barn and dangled a long piece of straw in front of the cats. Minerva—I had named the gray cat Minerva—batted at it with her paw. Pretty soon I didn't have the energy even for that anymore, and I shuffled back in.

"Are you feeling any better?" Mama asked when I came into the kitchen.

I shrugged.

"Maybe you better not go to school tomorrow either. Maybe I'd better make a doctor's appointment."

I sighed. I knew in my heart that my fate was sealed. Things weren't ever going to go back to the way they had been before. "No. I may as well go. I think I'll feel good enough tomorrow."

I slowly climbed the stairs to my room and got ready for bed. I sat by my window for a long time, looking out, thinking of something Grammy always said in the face of a trying situation. She always said, "Crying don't get the oil changed."

Probably she was right.

ADJUSTMENTS

The next day, I tracked Ivy Blake down at recess. She was sitting on the bleachers by the ball field watching some kids kick a soccer ball around.

"Hey," I said.

"Hey."

"I'm Prairie."

"I know."

I knew she knew, but I didn't know what else to say. I stared off across the ball field. "You want to play soccer or something?" I asked after a minute.

Ivy shook her head. "Not with them out there."

I saw what she meant. We were pretty much the two lowest kids on the totem pole in our classroom, along with Charlie, who wore a hearing aid, and Sasha, who barely spoke English. I thought a little and then I said, "Do you want to go swing on the swings then?" There was nobody over there.

She shrugged. Then she said, "Okay."

"So how'd you get your name?" she asked while we were swinging slowly back and forth, the chains squeaking. "I never heard Prairie as a name before."

"It was my mama's idea. She thought it was pretty."

"It is."

"How'd you get yours?"

"I don't know," Ivy said. "Nobody ever said."

I nodded like that made sense but it sounded sad to me. I twisted my swing until the chains wouldn't twist anymore, and then spun the twist out as fast as I could.

"So where're you from, anyway?" Ivy asked, twisting her chain too.

"North Carolina. My family has lived there for a long time. Forever."

"I never met anyone with a real southern accent before."

"I never knew anybody with a northern accent. Not before we moved here."

She grinned, and right at that moment I thought maybe we could be friends.

"Jamie Smith says you're a full-blooded Indian. Are you?"

I slid my eyes sideways at her. "Why? Does it matter?"

"I just thought it was sort of interesting. If it was true."

I pushed myself off harder and swung deeper and longer, and stretched out flat and tipped my head backward so I was looking at the school building upside down. "I'm not a full-blooded anything."

"I'm mostly Polish, I guess. That's what my aunt Connie said. But other stuff too. Irish and English and German, I think."

"Daddy says we're who knows what. All kinds of things. Including Cherokee. Probably. We're not in the tribe or anything. We're just—us. But my great-grandma Evers was part Cherokee, and there was Cherokee on the Vine side of my father's family too. That's the story that got handed down anyway. My grammy always said it was the truth as far as she knew."

"Uh-huh," Ivy said. I couldn't tell what she thought. She pushed back to get ready for a big swooping swing, but then the bell rang and we jumped off the swings and ran to get in line to troop back into school again.

18

SPEECH, SPEECH!

That afternoon Mrs. Hanson told us that in two days we were each going to have to give a speech about something we were interested in. Everybody groaned, me included.

I decided right away I'd give my speech on chickens, and it was easy to think of what I'd say. But it was not so easy to imagine saying it to a room full of people. The idea made me nervous. I didn't want to make a fool of myself in front of the whole classroom. That evening while I waited for Mama to get done with her class at the Arts Center, I looked up

"How to Give a Speech" on the computer at the library. I read a bunch of articles and I even watched a few videos.

It seemed pretty easy. Mrs. Hanson had said to be confident and friendly and take a deep breath before beginning to talk, which the articles said too. They also said to have an interesting story to tell, and not to apologize for making a mistake unless it was something really important. You were supposed to arrive early and make sure the microphone was working. Of course that didn't apply to me, but I knew I could do everything else they advised: Practice. Be enthusiastic. Make eye contact. Smile.

The day of the speeches I volunteered to go first, mostly to get it over with.

Mrs. Hanson stood before the class at a lectern she had dragged from the back of the room. She said, "I'm pleased to introduce Ms. Prairie Evers as our first speaker. She's going to tell us a little bit about raising chickens."

I gave Mrs. Hanson a polite nod and walked up the aisle. I hoped it didn't show that my legs were wobbling. At the lectern I reached out to shake her hand—the computer said to do that—and Mrs. Hanson looked surprised but she did reach out and shake my hand back.

I planted my feet. I took a deep breath. I set my index cards of notes on the lectern—notes in just single words, not full sentences, that's what the advice said—and put my arms up there too. I looked at the audience—not all at once, but a person here and there around the room—and took another deep breath, and commenced.

It went all right, I guess. I got from start to finish in about two minutes, which was only about three times as quick as I intended. My voice squeaked here and there and I forgot what some of the words on my index cards meant—like *soup* and *wdshvings*—and I made a sweeping movement and brushed all the cards to the floor at one point. I had to stop and gather them back up, but I didn't apologize. I just kept plowing forward. Then the best part of the speech came. I ran to the window and signaled to Daddy that it was time. Mrs. Hanson frowned in a puzzled way but I just smiled confidently and said, "I have a visual aid. It's coming now."

Mrs. Hanson raised her eyebrows. I ran to the classroom door and opened it for Daddy. He was carrying Fiddle in a cage, and Fiddle was not happy. He was croaking and spluttering and hissing. I suddenly understood what the phrase *spitting mad* really meant. I don't know why I hadn't thought of such an adventure striking him so amiss. It seemed like a good idea the day before when I talked Daddy into it. I admit I didn't tell Daddy the whole story, but had only described our speeches as a show-and-tell day. I cleared my throat. I said, "This is my daddy. And this is my rooster, Fiddle." I looked at my notes. They didn't say anything, because I'd expected this part of the presentation to carry itself off on sheer interest value.

"I, uh—"

Suddenly I couldn't think what to say. Half the kids started whispering and laughing, which made me freeze up even more.

"I—"

The talking and laughing got louder and more excited. Pretty soon Mrs. Hanson was going to have to come up and take over. I didn't want that.

"I raised him from when he was a baby," I said, and opened the cage door.

19

FLYING FIDDLE

Fiddle didn't come out, so I leaned down and looked in at him. I wiggled my pencil in front of his face to get his attention, and suddenly he came charging out like the pencil was a snake he had to protect the hens from. I yanked my pencil back, but Fiddle just kept coming. He ran smack into Chrissy Jones, who sits in front in the center aisle. She shrieked and Fiddle panicked. He ran down the aisle, and when he couldn't find a way out, he began flapping his wings, which caused everyone in the two rows on either side of him to shove out of their desks in alarm. Half the girls were squealing, and almost all the boys were *cock-a-doodle-dooing*.

I headed toward Fiddle, but he turned and ran back up the row, flapping all the way, and somehow he got up enough speed to lift off. He landed on the lectern. I took one step toward him and he made another desperate flight onto Mrs. Hanson's desk. Daddy and I glanced at each other and began to go toward him from opposite sides. Daddy was speaking softly, trying to calm him, but Fiddle was too worked up to listen. He flapped his wings again and made it up onto the wide shelf that runs above the blackboard. He landed right next to the globe Mrs. Hanson keeps stored up there, and then, to my horror, he pooped.

Everyone in the room was shouting now except for me and Daddy and Mrs. Hanson and maybe Ivy Blake. Fiddle must have felt safe up on that shelf, or else he was just out of options. He sat there staring down at us, his chest heaving. His eyes were very bright. Mrs. Hanson tried to quiet the room down, saying "Class, quiet now" in her most no-nonsense voice. Daddy took his flannel overshirt off real slow and nodded toward Fiddle to tell me we should advance real careful toward him. "Hey, Fiddle," I said in a gentle singsong voice. "It's all right. It's just me and Daddy. Nobody's going to hurt you. Don't try and fly now. Just sit still. Daddy'll take you home if you sit still."

Daddy followed right behind me and then with a soft, quick motion, he reached up and grabbed Fiddle's ankles. Fiddle exploded in a fit, but Daddy kept a good hold and pulled him down under his arm to pin his wings in and draped his overshirt over him and somehow he got him contained. Then before Fiddle knew what was happening, Daddy shoved him back into the cage and latched the door behind him.

The kids erupted again. There was whispering and laughing and shouting and clapping and *cock-a-doodle-dooing* and someone yelled, "Yeah, Fiddle! My man!"

Daddy draped his shirt over the cage and looked at me inquiringly. I knew what that look meant. It meant, *I think that's enough now. Don't you?*

I gave him a weak smile. I cleared my throat. I said, quickly and as loud as I could to be heard over the noise, "Chickens are a fine animal to raise, they are friendly and interesting, they are a moneymaker, and you will find yourself getting more and more interested in them every day, once you begin. Thank you. And thank you, Daddy. I think we are done."

He nodded at Mrs. Hanson, who nodded faintly at him in return, and picked up Fiddle's cage and left. To my surprise, the kids began shouting "Good-bye, Fiddle! Come back again!"

Mrs. Hanson said, "Well." She cleared her throat. "That was certainly very—interesting."

I turned red. I said, "Thank you, ma'am."

"If anyone else has a visual aid, I think they'd better run it past me first. And Prairie, climb up on a chair and clean off that shelf before you sit down."

"Yes, ma'am," I said. I could hear a lot of whispering and giggling as I wiped off the shelf, but when I walked back to my seat, a bunch of the boys started clapping and whistling through their teeth again. Aaron Childs even raised a hand in a high five to slap mine as I walked by. Things hadn't gone exactly as I'd planned, but probably Grammy would've said that letting nature take its course was the best idea anyway.

THE TRAIL OF TEARS

Amabelle was the next volunteer, and she gave a speech about her family's trip to the Grand Canyon that didn't get anywhere near the applause mine did. She finished and sat down, and then Chrissy Jones went, and then Aaron Childs. When Mrs. Hanson asked for another volunteer after that, nobody moved for a minute. But then Ivy Blake stood up and walked to the front of the room like she was walking to her doom. She got behind the lectern and stared down at the papers she'd carried with her.

"This speech is called 'The Trail of Tears,'" she said. "It's about Cherokee Indians."

I sat up straight.

Ivy cleared her throat. I could see her hands shake.

"Very terrible things have happened in pretty places like North Carolina," Ivy read. "When the white people first came here, they brought diseases with them. Right away a disease called smallpox killed a lot of Indian people. It killed half the Cherokees. The Cherokees lived in what is now the states of Georgia and North and South Carolina."

There was a long pause while Ivy swallowed hard. I stared at her hands, willing them to stop shaking, but they didn't.

Ivy cleared her throat again. "When Andrew Jackson got elected president, things got even worse for the Cherokees. They got sent away from their land, which was the most terrible thing of all. They loved their land. They were farmers and hunters who lived in the Smoky Mountains. They had lived there for a long time, but Mr. Jackson made them leave."

I knew that; Grammy often spoke of it. There was no love lost between her and Mr. Jackson, although he was long dead before Grammy arrived on earth.

"In the winter of 1838 the Cherokee people got rounded up and marched out of their homes and into the territory of Oklahoma. Fifteen thousand people were rounded up and marched off. Maybe more."

As Ivy spoke, I tried to imagine all those folks walking in a long line toward Oklahoma, walking a thousand miles in the winter. I wished I had been there with my rifle when the soldiers came. But probably it wouldn't have done any good.

"They weren't supposed to have to go. The Supreme Court said they didn't. But President Jackson made his soldiers round them up anyway. Some people were cooking food they had to leave on the fire. They had to leave their dogs with just a pat on the head. Most of them never even had time to get a blanket or put on their shoes."

I sat very still, listening. I reckoned those were terrible times, times that put my sassing against going to school to shame.

"A lot of the people died on the way. Thousands and thousands. They were hungry and cold and worn out, walking all that way with no warm clothes and almost nothing to eat. That's why it's called the Trail of Tears."

It surprised me how quiet the room was. Ivy cleared her throat again, and even though she was doing such a good job, her voice was shaky.

"There was some good news too. A few of the Cherokees kept away from the soldiers. They stayed hidden in the hills of North Carolina. They are now called the Eastern Band of Cherokee."

I nodded. Those were some of my people, or so it was always said in my family.

"And the people who made it to Oklahoma set themselves up as a nation again and started over. They had an alphabet thought up by a man named Sequoyah, and a constitution and a government and a newspaper and schools."

Right after Ivy said that, she seemed to freeze, like she suddenly realized what she was doing: standing up in front of the class giving a speech. She took a deep wavering breath and said, kind of sudden, "The end."

She'd been reading from her papers all along without ever looking up, which the computer said not to do, but it was a good speech anyway. Right after she said "The end," she darted a look at me. Then she sat down.

When the next speech started (Randy Curtis talking about his favorite computer game, which was not interesting at all), I took the chance to pass Ivy a note. We're not supposed to do that, but it was important. My situation was nowhere near as severe as that of the folks marching off on the Trail of Tears, but I had marched into a new territory in New Paltz, New York, and Ivy was the first person to act like a friend toward me.

Dear Ivy,
    That was a good speech. Do you want to eat lunch together?

                              Your friend (if you want),
                              Prairie Evers

21

IVY'S MAMA

After that, Ivy and I always ate lunch together
and played together at recess. One day we came
up with the idea that we'd wear the same kind of
clothes the next day. We'd wear red sweatshirts and
white tennis shoes and blue jeans. We decided to
act the same and speak the same the whole day too.
When Ivy leaned her chin on her hand, I leaned my
chin on my hand. When I waved my arm to answer
a question, Ivy waved her same arm, and when Ivy
stood up, I stood up too.

I guess neither one of us ever had a friend who

was just about a twin before. We started giggling in the middle of reading time when it was quiet all over the room, and we could not stop. We were spluttering and sniffling, trying to keep those giggles pent up, but they wouldn't stay pent. Even after Mrs. Hanson said, "Ivy, Prairie, that's enough," we still couldn't stop.

Then she said, "Go clap out the erasers from now until the bell rings. Get them good and clean."

I said, "Yes, ma'am, Mrs. Hanson, but I have to catch my bus."

"You've got time. Go and clap out the erasers."

Ivy and I got to laughing at the puffs of chalk tickling our noses, and at the smell of it, like a hundred blackboards with a hundred teachers writing all at once. One thing led to another and we didn't get done until after the bell announcing the end of the day had rung. We ran the erasers back to Mrs. Hanson and gathered our things from our lockers as quick as we could, but the bus pulled off from the curb without me.

"Oh no!" It was a long way to walk home, and even if I did try, I'd never get there before dark. Besides which, Mama and Daddy wouldn't want me walking anyway. "I'm sunk." I stared at Ivy with big eyes.

She squeezed my hand. "You can come home with me. We'll call your folks from there."

"But Mama is at the Arts Center, and Daddy's probably outside."

"Well then, my mom will give you a ride. It'll be okay."

I saw she was right, and headed home with her. It was a kind of adventure to walk through the streets of the town, and my spirits began to rise. When we got there, though, I was set back again.

Ivy's house was painted dark brown and frowned at you with a "keep away" feeling. It was crammed in between two others that weren't any more cheerful, and the yard was cluttered with broken-down things. Inside, Ivy's mama was sitting at the table flipping through a magazine. She looked up when we came in, but even though I'd never met her before, she didn't say anything.

Ivy is pretty. She has long yellow hair that falls straight as a pencil down her back, clear to her waist. She has green eyes with a little rim of brown around the edge of them, like a pond. She's got just a few freckles across her nose, and when you're talking to her, she sits up real straight and quiet and watches you steady with those deepwater eyes so you know she's really listening. You'd think her mama would be pretty too, but she wasn't. She was the skinniest lady I ever saw, and her eyes didn't have any smiling in them.

She wasn't nice like Ivy, either. She just flipped through her magazine like we weren't even there. That's what she must've spent most of her time doing, because she had magazines stacked up halfway to the ceiling in one corner. I thought to myself that if she saved the money it cost each month to buy them, she could've given Ivy something nice. Some ribbons or barrettes for her hair, maybe. Ivy had such pretty hair and no ribbon or band that was special to put in it.

Ivy didn't seem surprised that her mama didn't say anything. She said, "Mom, this is my friend Prairie. She missed her bus. I told her she could call her folks from here, or else we could give her a ride home, is that all right?"

Her mama gave a little put-upon laugh, like Ivy was forever asking things of her. She flipped her magazine shut and snuffed out her cigarette. Then she shoved up out of her chair and grabbed her jacket off the back of it and said, "Come on then," and headed to the door.

Ivy said, "We better hurry up."

"I could just call home. Mama might be there by now, or Daddy might've come inside for a drink of water or a sandwich," I whispered, but Ivy just shook her head.

Ivy's mama's car was little and lime green, with chrome wheels. The steering wheel had a laced-up leather cover, and so did the stick shift. Once upon a time it had been brand-new and exciting, you could tell. But that had been a long, long time ago. Now everything about it looked faded and old. Still, when Ivy's mama turned on the ignition, the car said *vroom*, just like in a cartoon. I confess it gave me a start. Ivy's mama peeled away from the curb, and the car raced down the street. I clutched onto Ivy's hand for a second.

The backseat was so tiny, it might as well have not even been there, but Ivy and me sat squished into it together. We talked a little, but not like usual. When we got to my house, my mama was coming down the drive. She said, "Prairie, where have you been?"

"I missed the bus. This is my friend Ivy. Her mama was kind enough to drive me home."

Mama leaned down and looked in through the car window. "My goodness, thank you."

"That's all right," Ivy's mama said, and you could tell it really wasn't.

Mama looked at Ivy. "It's nice to meet you. Prairie's told me all about you. You'll have to come to supper one night soon."

Ivy said, "That would be nice."

Mama looked over at Mrs. Blake. "How about Friday? Ivy can ride the bus home with Prairie, and we'll drop her off home sometime Saturday. Is five o'clock too late?"

Ivy's mama looked taken aback, but she said, slowlike, "I guess that'd be okay."

Ivy and I scrambled out of the car and jumped up and down and hugged each other real quick. Then Ivy got in the front seat. I waved until the car was out of sight.

I was happy Ivy was coming over Friday to spend the night, but even so, I felt quiet after she left. I wished I could talk to Grammy.

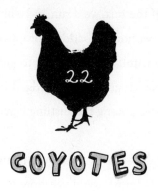

COYOTES

Pretty soon I couldn't imagine a day when I didn't have Ivy as my friend. Her mama let her spend all kinds of time with me, and Ivy came to my house after school nine days out of ten. I hardly went back to her place after that first time. Ivy didn't ask, and I was just as glad.

I was amazed at how we liked all the same things: pepperoni pizza, RC Cola, swimming, singing, and playing Monopoly. We both wanted a pair of in-line roller skates but didn't think we'd ever get them. Also, neither one of us was exactly popular in school. Ivy was too quiet and wary, and I was too flat-out strange. But we didn't care, we had each other.

When we got off the bus, we'd run and climb up into the big maple beside the henhouse. Daddy'd propped an old wooden ladder against the trunk so it was easy to get to the platform of planks he'd nailed together and wedged into the tree's big fork. Sitting up there among the rustling leaves was one of our favorite things.

We'd talk and talk—mostly about the future. From on high it seemed as if we almost could see how our lives would be. I'd keep on at the farm as my folks did, only I wanted to have a horse to ride around, too. Ivy wanted to be a ballet dancer, and have a dog, and maybe be a famous movie director one day. She said now that she knew a little bit about chickens, she'd probably have a flock of those too, although how she'd fit that in with ballet dancing I couldn't quite see. But she did love the chickens and had a way with them. I think they liked how quiet and calm she was. The chicken I named Smoke in particular had taken a shine to Ivy and followed her around like a puppy.

After a while we'd go play with the cats, or swing on the tire swing, or build forts out of hay bales up in the mow and pretend we were Wild West cowboys or Cherokee Indians. Sometimes we pretended we were orphan princesses running a great kingdom together. Other times we just hiked back along the lane to the woods to see what we could see. Every afternoon we fed

Fiddle and the hens, gathered the eggs, and set out food for the coyote who showed up sometimes way at the edge of the woods, so he'd leave the chickens alone. We put out fruit and vegetables that had gotten old, and mice Mama had caught in traps in the house.

"A coyote loves a mouse to eat. I believe it's like a chocolate bar to you or me," I told Ivy one day as we hiked toward the woods. I had two of them in a plastic sack. It was sad for them, but they had been in the wrong place at the wrong time, and they were going to make quite a treat for some lucky coyote.

Ivy said, "Yuck," but she kept tromping along with me. "That's just hard to believe."

"They'll eat all kinds of things. Fruit and fish and vegetables and grass, and sometimes something big, like a deer."

"And people's animals. You hear about that."

"Not very often. They know it's dangerous, going near people."

"How do you know so much about it?"

"I don't know." Even with Ivy I didn't admit how much learning I'd always done on my own out of sheer curiosity. I'd found out in school that it was safer to keep quiet about some things. Probably Ivy wouldn't have minded, but I didn't like to take the chance. Besides, it seemed to me like knowing about coyotes was just natural, like breathing. "I learned a lot of it from my grammy, and from Daddy too, I guess."

"Oh."

I cut my eyes sideways at her. Sometimes it struck me how Ivy didn't have any family that I knew of besides her mama. Her mama didn't seem worth the powder to blow her up to me, and every time I thought about it, I got worried.

It wasn't something we talked about, though. In truth, the thought of talking about it made me nervous. It was easier to go on talking about coyotes. "It's a desperate coyote who'll eat a man's stock, Daddy says. He says a coyote has got to eat, same as you and me. I reckon he's in the minority in his way of thinking on that. Daddy admits coyotes will devour chickens if they get a chance and there's not something else about for them to eat. But he says they're as good as a cat for pest control, they do love a mouse so. And he says they're a good family-values animal, the government ought to promote them as a model for folks to look up to instead of encouraging people to hunt them down."

Ivy nodded, and there was something lonesome about it. Maybe I had said *Daddy* too many times in a row. Sometimes I trod on Ivy's feelings without meaning to. I decided to hold my tongue for a while, which was not the easiest thing in the world, but I did it for Ivy's sake.

That night, after she went home, I sat at the kitchen table and thought about everything I knew about coyotes.

Coyotes marry for life. They have their babies in the spring, and the babies don't leave the den their mama has made until they are three weeks of age. Then they do go outside of it, but just a little ways. When they're older, the mama and daddy and aunts and uncles teach the pups to hunt. They are handing over the things the pups will need to know as they go on in life. Coyotes move away from their home place when they are grown, but they don't go too far.

A person will hear a coyote more often than she sees him. When they howl, they might seem to be in one place when really they're somewhere else. It's something to do with the way their voice carries through the air. I've practiced throwing my own voice, but so far I haven't been able to do it. In the fall if you hear them, it's probably a mama calling out to her pups. She's checking on them. She gives them some free rein, but really she doesn't think they're quite grown yet, so she calls out, "Where are you and what are you doing?" They call back to her, all together, saying, "Yes, Mama, here we are, we are all right."

I'll bet five dollars that sometimes those pups are getting into one kind of trouble or another. I'll wager they don't say the whole of it to their mama and so get off scot-free with some of their exploits.

A coyote can get used to about anything. They are alert and wary, careful in their habits. They can run fast and far. Coyotes help raise up their sister's children and vice versa. There's always someone to depend on if something happens to the mama or daddy.

All in all, a coyote's ways are good to know. I wrote them all down for Ivy. My information was something she could carry with her. I thought some of it could come in useful to her, because in truth it seemed to me Ivy might've done better to be raised by a family of coyotes for as much attention as her mama seemed to pay to her.

23

PUP

The gray cat Minerva had babies in October, and I let Ivy name her favorite one. She called it Pup. Pup was smoke colored with a white dot on the top of his head and had large feet like a puppy does before it has grown into dog size. I didn't say a thing to anyone, but I had it in my mind to send Pup home with Ivy the minute he was old enough. That would be at eight weeks of age, so he could go with her at Christmas.

I got Mama to take me to town on a day when Ivy wasn't with me, thinking to spend some of my egg money on a collar. I thought it would set Pup off, giftlike. I picked out a red collar in the store, thinking it would look handsome against his gray fur.

Mama came up beside me and said, "What's that you've got there?"

"It's a collar for Pup. I'm going to give him to Ivy for a present." Mama got a funny look on her face, and I thought maybe she didn't like me to give away one of our own without asking. Maybe she was attached to Pup herself. "Is that all right?"

"Oh, Prairie." Mama put her arm around my shoulders.

"Isn't it all right? Ivy likes him in particular."

"I'm going to tell you this plainly. I don't think Ivy's mama will let her have a kitten."

"Why not?"

"Oh, honey. Ivy's mama just strikes me as very unhappy. Very—closed off."

"Selfish, you mean. And mean."

"Well—" Mama looked pained. She doesn't like to speak unkindly of anyone, no matter how much they deserve it. "I don't know about that. But I can't imagine her saying okay to a kitten. I just can't. I'm sorry."

"How about a fish then?" I had a kind of hard time blurting it out, I so wanted to give Ivy that kitten. A fish isn't the same as a cat, but it's something living to take notice of and maybe give notice of you in return. Fish are peaceful and quiet, maybe Ivy would like that.

But Mama said real soft, "I don't think so, Prairie. I don't think her mother would allow it."

I started to get angry then; it seemed like she was saying no just to say it. "Why not?" I said, quite loud. "That's dumb. A fish doesn't bother anyone."

An old lady who was looking at tinned cat food glanced over to see what the ruckus was about. Mama didn't take any notice of her. She hunkered down and put her hands on my shoulders. "Prairie Evers, you're a good friend to think of giving Ivy such nice gifts. She could use a friend at home like Pup, or even a fish. But trust me when I say her mama won't allow it. It would only upset Ivy. That's why I'm telling you no."

I bit my bottom lip. I'm not much of a crybaby but I felt like I had lost my last friend in the world. I don't know why. I wasn't the one who had lost something; Ivy was and she didn't even know it, so how could it hurt her? That's the way I felt, anyway.

Mama said, "Sometimes the truth is a real sad thing."

I didn't say anything. I didn't want to bawl right there in the pet supplies aisle.

"Can you think of some other gift you'd like to get Ivy? Maybe a game?"

I shook my head. Anybody could give a game. I wanted something special. Then I did think of something and I said, "Maybe."

Mama took my hand. "Come on and show me. I'll help you buy it if you haven't got enough."

115

I wasn't aggravated with her anymore, but I wanted to look for Ivy's present by myself. "I've got enough. I know what I'll get, it's not something living."

"All right then. You meet me at the checkout in ten minutes."

What I did was get some pretty things for Ivy's hair. I got her ribbons and headbands and barrettes and all manner of things because her hair is so pretty and she didn't have any of those things. It was a gift that was useful and special at the same time, and that seemed right to me.

When I came up behind Mama at the checkout, she was carrying a big old ivy in a clay pot. She didn't say anything about it until we were in the truck. Daddy was driving and I sat in between them like always. Mama was hidden behind that big plant.

"You know I did a lot of rambling around before I met your daddy," she said.

I kept quiet. It didn't seem like a question, really.

"I left home the minute I graduated high school. I couldn't wait to get gone. I must've broken my mother's heart."

I kept quiet some more.

"I found out pretty quickly that life can get hard and lonesome on your own, but I was too proud to go running back home. And then I met your daddy." She smiled across at him. "He was such a kind person. My parents never did take the trouble to get to know him like they should have."

I kept quiet again because it seemed like she was talking to Daddy more than me.

"The day I met him at the craft fair in Asheville was a great day in my life."

"And you bought one of his birdhouses, even though you didn't have a yard or anywhere to put it. You just rented a room in a house in Asheville, above the café where you were washing dishes. A room that only had one little bitty window that looked over some rooftops." I knew this part of the story by heart.

"That's right. And when I lived there by myself, without a friend or relation within five hundred miles, I learned that a plant can be good company. A plant is something to care for. It needs you. It's company, funny as that might seem."

"It doesn't seem funny to me." I grabbed hold of Mama's hand and held it tight.

"I got this for Ivy," she said. "It's her namesake."

Daddy put his arm across me and laid a hand on Mama's shoulder. We rode on home like that.

I was glad we got Ivy those gifts. I believed she would like them. But still I didn't like to think of her falling asleep at night in her bed without Pup curled in beside her. I will tell you what I did not tell Mama. I got that red collar because I was determined to make Pup Ivy's own, even if she couldn't haul him home with her.

24

SILVER LINING

Since Mama was pretty certain Ivy wouldn't be able to take Pup home, I figured I didn't have to wait for Christmas to give him to her. I told myself that was the silver lining in the cloud. Grammy always told me to look for the good even in bad situations. It's a challenge, but pretty often you can find something if you look hard.

Not always, though. I'd looked and looked for the good in Grammy moving back to Vine's Cove, but I couldn't see it. I could've put "meeting Ivy" in the good column, only I didn't see why Grammy would've had to leave for me to do that. It seemed like Mama and Daddy were going to send me to school anyway. I could've put "getting mail in the mailbox," which I did love, but I'd have loved Grammy being here in person even better. I could've put "chickens" down on the silver-lining list, but I might have thought of that anyway.

Then again, I might not.

So I guess that's it, the silver lining in my cloud of Grammy's moving: my hens and Fiddle. Even on the worst day you ever had—a day when your favorite shirt's in the wash and you almost miss the bus because you spent so much time looking for it, a day when your best friend misses school because she's got the flu—it's hard not to get a kick out of a chicken.

It's just like I imagined. Every morning Fiddle crows at sunrise, crows and crows until it's full light, and I love that. I can't imagine the day beginning without it. I can't imagine the flock without Fiddle at all. The way he acts, so proud and sure, you'd think he'd invented the whole world and then put himself in charge of it.

The hens spend their time scratching around the yard and Fiddle is always nearby, watching over them. They have their arguments about who is who, and Fiddle marches over to settle it. If there's the shadow of a hawk swooping overhead, or even just a butterfly, he rounds them up and herds them all to safety. Then when the danger seems past, he goes back to scouting for bugs and grubs. When he finds something, he shepherds the hens to the feast like a gentleman instead of gobbling it up himself, and they set into eating as if they'd never encountered food before. Another scuffle erupts, Fiddle settles it, the hens settle down, and everyone goes back to thinking about lunch.

I love the fact that they will go on this way forever, doing the same things every day. And every day I get the same thrill out of it.

When I gather the eggs each afternoon I feel like I've really done something, no matter that it's really them who've done the work. And at night when I let them back in the coop to roost—counting to make sure I've got everyone, because the hen I named Sneaky likes to stay out if she can, which isn't safe even though I do leave food out for the coyote—I shut the door real soft and then stand there for a minute, listening to them shift around as they get ready for the night. It makes me feel peaceful. Chickens are just themselves, without ever trying to be anything else. I'll bet it's the same way with a dog or a cat or a hamster even.

That's what I was thinking when I said to Ivy after supper the next Friday night, "I want Pup to be your cat. I think he ought to be, you love him so much and he loves you too. He hardly pays any mind to me at all." I exaggerated a little to be sure she wouldn't argue with me.

"I don't think—" Ivy began, but I cut in.

"I've got too many cats already and I'm afraid this one might not ever grow into those big clumsy feet."

"That's really nice of you, but—"

"You'd be doing me a favor, taking the responsibility for this cat off my hands," I said firmly.

She went still then, and hugged Pup to her and buried her face in his fur. When she looked up, her eyes were bright, like she was going to cry. "My mom will never let me have a cat. Never, not in a million years. I won a fish at the fair one time and it even came in its own tiny fishbowl and she wouldn't let me keep it. She made me give it to the neighbor."

I was glad Mama had prepared me for this. I shrugged, as if this was no tragedy but just the usual way of things. "Well, Pup will just have to stay here then. But I don't want to be the one who is his owner. He is *not* my cat. I've got too many cats. He's yours."

"Really?" Ivy looked as if I had just handed her the moon on a silver platter.

"I just said so, didn't I?"

Ivy flopped down on the floor and started dragging a string around for Pup to chase. "I'm going to teach him to fetch," she said. "I'm going to find a little rubber ball, or a catnip mouse, and start training him."

"You can't teach a cat to fetch!"

"Bet I can." She wasn't paying any attention to me. She wiggled the string and Pup leaped onto it with his paws splayed out and his tail twitching. "Good kitty," she whispered. Pup started purring as loud as a freight train.

I watched them and felt very satisfied. Partly I was just happy that Ivy was happy. But also I was proud of myself for arranging this for Ivy. Right that minute I started making another plan for something I knew Ivy should do, something that she so far had resisted.

HUNTING

Later that night Ivy and I made new signs for my eggs, to advertise them better. That was Ivy's idea. FRESH FARM EGGS, we wrote out in shadow-box letters that we colored in with all different shades of markers. SPECIAL! $4.00 A DOZEN! (Four dollars is what we always charged, but Ivy was right, it looked more interesting with the word *special* out front.) We made tags for each dozen that said EGGS BY TILLIE, EGGS BY ELMIRA, EGGS BY SNOWBALL. We didn't really know whose eggs were whose—it was impossible to tell because we almost never caught them actually laying—but it was close enough to the truth and we thought people would get a kick out of it.

Before bed we watched for the coyote at the far edge of the woods and caught sight of him eating what we left. Then we stayed up late, scaring each other crazy with ghost stories. It was just a day like any other, really. But I had my plan for Ivy and I was set on making it happen.

The next morning I set in to badgering her about going hunting, which is something she's never wanted to do. I'd been plaguing her about it for weeks. I knew she'd like it, if only she'd give it a chance.

So that day I set in again, and after a while she said, "Fine. We'll go."

"You're going to love this, you'll see." I ran to get my BB gun.

"We won't shoot anything living," I said as we headed out to the back pasture. "We'll pretend to be girls who live in olden times and make our way in the wilderness." I pointed at the bale of straw. "Pretend that's a bear come to harm us, or a highway robber, or a deer we need to eat."

Ivy nodded, but she didn't look happy. I shrugged that off and took aim and fired. Ivy flinched. I had hit my mark, for I'm a fair shot, and I turned to her, grinning. She was paler than ever.

"Here, you try." I held the gun out toward her.

Ivy crossed her arms over her chest and shook her head.

I stomped my foot. "You're just being stubborn. Everybody

ought to know how to handle a gun. How many people have got a friend who's willing to show them?"

Ivy didn't answer, and that made me even madder. "You're acting like a coward. I'm surprised at you! I thought you had some gumption."

Ivy gave me a furious look, and she tore that gun from me. She was shaking like a poplar leaf. I felt sorry then for being so harsh. I said, gently, "Ivy, you've got to learn this. What if a band of outlaws came upon us and we weren't ready for them? What if we were a Cherokee family trying to elude the soldiers?"

"There's no band of outlaws coming. And we're not Cherokees hiding from soldiers." Ivy's skin seemed stretched tight across the bones of her face.

I sighed. "I know that, but we're pretending. You like pretending."

"Not about stuff like this." Ivy said that so softly, I didn't think I could have heard her right.

"Here, come on, I'll teach you how to shoot." It's easy, more or less, you just pull the trigger. You can learn to take aim before you fire, but I thought it best just to get her started.

What Ivy did next I would not have predicted. It made me uneasy, I confess. She took that gun and lifted it up in the air. She looked at me real brief, a kind of wild look, and then she fired. She fired and fired and fired.

There are a lot of bullets in a BB gun if you have filled it up, all you have to do is keep cocking the trigger and pulling it back.

Ivy fired up into the sky until the gun wouldn't shoot anymore. Then she flung it down and went running across the fields. She was half out of sight before I thought to run after her.

I never did catch her. Ivy ran too fast. I finally gave up and went and picked up the gun and walked home, feeling put out. We had been going to play all day and had packed a lunch even. There were cheese sandwiches with pickles on them, and chocolate chip cookies, and two RC Colas, our favorite and a special treat. Mama didn't buy soda very often, and now I didn't even want mine.

IVY'S DADDY

When I got back, Ivy was beside the hen-house. I said, "Hey," and she did too.

I asked, "Are you okay?" She said she was. "Well then, what do you want to do?"

"I don't know."

I wasn't feeling very cheerful after she had just run off like that.

Ivy said, "What do *you* want to do?"

I shrugged. Then I climbed up into the maple tree. I didn't know if I wanted Ivy to climb up after me or not, but she did. After a while we spoke of this and that. We were somewhat strained, but Ivy and I don't have it in us to hold a grudge for long.

Suddenly Ivy blurted out, "I have to tell you something."

I held out for a moment and then I said, "What?"

"It's about my father."

Ivy had never mentioned her father before. I'd never asked. It seemed like if her daddy was no more use than her mama, it wouldn't be something she'd want to talk about much.

"I don't have one," she said.

I was thankful to be sitting down when she told me why. If I'd been standing, I believe I would have fallen under the weight of it.

"My mother killed my father. She shot him," she said.

I was so surprised, I couldn't even move.

"I was five. I was there."

"What happened?" I whispered.

"They had a big fight. I don't know what it was about. But they were *so* mad at each other. They weren't themselves. That's what my aunt Connie always told me. They were drinking, I guess. I don't remember that part. I heard yelling and stuff being thrown."

I flinched. "That must have been scary."

Ivy nodded. Her eyes were big and bright, but she didn't cry. I don't know how she goes about each day, what with all that happened. She is stronger than she looks with that fair skin and long yellow hair and her quiet ways.

"Why did she do it?" I asked.

"I don't know. She was just so mad, they both were. It was an accident. A bad mistake. It happened so fast. In just one moment she did something she couldn't take back." Ivy looked like she was a million miles away. "They were young and they let their tempers get away from them. That's what Aunt Connie said."

I wondered where Aunt Connie was now. "But—" I didn't know how to say what I thought. Tripping on a tree root and dropping your gun and having it go off, that was maybe an accident. Pulling the trigger while the gun was loaded and pointed at somebody? That was something else.

"My dad was bigger than my mom, and she was afraid he would hurt her. He was throwing things at her. She was defending herself. That's what the court papers said. My aunt Connie explained it all to me."

I opened my mouth but nothing came out.

"It was called justifiable homicide."

We were sitting at the edge of the platform in the tree, swinging our legs and looking down at the ground below. I didn't know what to say, so I didn't say anything. I could see Ivy had spent some time reflecting on those words.

"My mother didn't get into trouble, not really. Not like you'd think."

I kept on not saying anything, looking at the toes of my boots swinging there below me in the leafy air.

"She had to go to classes for a long time. But she didn't go to jail."

I nodded, to show I was listening and I understood. I gave Ivy's toe a little kick with my toe, to show I thought as much of her as ever, and more. She gave my toe a little kick back. We were both real quiet for a time. I listened to my chickens down below, pecking about in the yard. They didn't sound any different than ever. I wondered how that could be, with what Ivy had just told me falling down through the air.

"My dad loved me," Ivy said. "I know he did. He gave me a Battleship game for Christmas the year before she shot him. He wrapped it up himself, I'll bet. I was too little for it, but I loved it. I remember the paper, it was white with red Santa Clauses on it."

"I'm sorry," I said.

"He's buried back where he grew up, near Schenectady. Aunt Connie took me to the funeral, but his family didn't want anything to do with us after what my mom did. I never saw any of them again."

"I'm really sorry, Ivy."

Ivy did cry then. She bent down her head and wept real quiet, with her shoulders shaking. I didn't know what to do. I just sat there beside her, kicking her toe with my toe every now and then. After a while Ivy wiped her face off with the back of her shirtsleeve and said, "We moved here afterward, from

Poughkeepsie. My mom didn't want everyone knowing. And plus my aunt Connie was here, so we moved in with her."

I thought to myself that was the one thing Ivy's mama had done that made sense. "So where's your aunt now?"

Ivy's whole body slumped. She looked even sadder than before, which I would not have thought possible. "She died last year. She had cancer."

"Oh, Ivy. That's not fair."

Ivy smiled kind of wobbly at that. "Yeah."

I had a feeling inside me like I wanted to go out and kick something.

"I never told anybody any of this before." Ivy looked sore afraid when she said that. "I've been worrying about telling you. I was afraid maybe you wouldn't like me anymore if you knew."

I grabbed her hand and squeezed it hard. I could feel it shaking. "That would never happen, Ivy. Never."

Ivy nodded and tears kept rolling down her cheeks, but her hand stopped shaking.

"I don't hate my mom," she said after a while. "She didn't used to be like she is now, so much. They were just so mad at each other that night. You know?"

I nodded, but I did not know.

"She's sorry but there's nothing she can do about it, so she pretends it didn't happen. But it eats away at her, you know?"

I nodded again. Ivy stared up into the branches and leaves above our heads. "I'm sorry I was no good at hunting."

"That's okay. It was a dumb idea."

I put the gun away in the mudroom that evening and never brought it out again when Ivy was there.

PATIENCE

I wrote Grammy another letter that night. I kept trying to talk her into using the neighbor's computer so I could send e-mails from school, but she always said a letter would reach her in just a few days, quicker than she'd bother traipsing the five miles over to the neighbor's place, so I might as well apply pencil to paper and quit pestering her.

When she wrote things like that—traipsing and pestering—I missed her and North Carolina more than ever. I missed the sound of people talking who sounded like me and used the words I'd use. I missed the green smell of North Carolina and the mist hovering over the mountaintops. I missed the rhododendron and the redbud trees and the burbling streams hurrying down Peabody Mountain, and most of all I just missed Grammy. No matter how much I loved Mama and Daddy and Ivy, there was still a hole in my world.

I sat down at the kitchen table after supper that night and wrote and told Grammy everything Ivy told me. I said that I wanted to bring Ivy home to live with me because in my opinion her mama was no use at all. Even before Ivy told me about her daddy I thought that. I told Grammy I thought Ivy would be much better off with us, and what if her mama got mad and decided to shoot a gun off again? I asked Grammy what she thought.

I expected her to answer straightaway, and she did. But also I expected her to send me a solution to Ivy's problems, and that she did not do.

Grammy wrote,

My dear Prairie,

I thank you for your letter. It is always a pleasure to hear from you. I am doing fine, I thank you for inquiring. My knee does give me some trouble but it is nothing I cannot rise above most days. Your great-uncle Tecumseh sends you a howdy back and thinks you must be growing into a fine young lady. I told him yes, you are, and if he ever came down off this mountain to ride a bus up north to see, he'd know for his own self.

You've told me of your friend Ivy and her troubles, and you may rest assured she will figure in my thoughts each day, and I will wish the best of all things for her. I believe you've done as right as you could, just to listen and grab hold of her hand when she was feeling leery. That's about all any of us can do.

I don't blame you for wanting to bring Ivy home with you, any sensible person would. But Prairie, child, I do not know as it will happen. You've posed a hard riddle as to what to do and I tell you plainly, I do not know the answer. I don't know as there is an answer. You won't like that. I can see a stubborn look blooming on your face. I know that look well and have only to glance in the looking glass at myself to find it! I will study on it further in case I can think of something. In the meantime, do as you have always done and go on being Ivy's friend.

Give my love to your mama and daddy.

Your grandma,
Patience Evers

Grammy always said Patience was a ridiculous name for a person who had not been born with much. But she said it was a skill you could learn if you really tried, and I reckoned that was what she was advising to me, to have patience. I am like my grammy, and not having an answer to things doesn't sit easy with me. But she said to try and live with it and I did, or anyway, I tried.

28

FALLING
IN LOVE

A week after Ivy told me about her daddy, something else happened. Her mama got a boyfriend.

His name was George, and Ivy said he was very medium. Medium height, medium weight, medium-colored hair. I think that's a color Crayola should add to their crayon box. It would mean something like brown and something like blond and nothing you'd remark on either way. Ivy said George and her mama had fallen in love. I couldn't picture it, but Ivy said it was so.

I wrote and told Grammy of it right away. She wrote back and said, "Well, isn't that nice." I could tell she felt the same as me. Somewhat uncertain.

I told Ivy I thought she should keep a close watch on the situation. "You probably should be nice to George, polite and all, but keep a close eye out. Listen to the things he says and see if you can tell which way the wind is blowing."

"Oh, I will."

"Remember the coyote."

"I will. Don't worry."

I was sure she would, for Ivy is no fool, but I decided I'd keep a close watch on things too. In a pack of coyotes, everyone watches out for one another: they are a team. It works that way with coyotes and cats and chickens, and I think it ought to work that way with people too.

29

MISCELLANEOUS

Vocabulary is my favorite subject in school. Mrs. Hanson has us play a game where each row is a team and our job is to think of synonyms for whatever word she puts up on the board. We're supposed to go as fast as we can and just shout the answers out. Mrs. Hanson writes all the answers in separate columns, and at the end of the game the row with the most words wins. Amabelle and I are the best players on our team.

One day after we won—again—I tapped her shoulder and whispered, "You have a nice name. It means lovable." I'd looked it up one day because it bothered me. It looked too much like *Annabelle* and I thought maybe her parents had just made a spelling mistake. But no, it really was a name.

She looked surprised, but she said, "Thanks."

"You're welcome. But it's nothing to thank me for, it's just true."

"Your name's kind of cool, too. It's different."

I grinned. "It is that."

"How'd you get it?"

"My mama. She thought it was a pretty word. She and my daddy had been out west on a camping trip before I came along, and she loved it there. She thought it was a name with a lot of space to it."

"Huh." She was going to say something else, but Mrs. Hanson stopped us.

"Amabelle! Prairie! Get back to work."

We ducked our heads and got busy. Our assignment was to write a letter to someone using our vocabulary words. That was easy—of course I was writing to Grammy. I told her about our game. I said,

We won on the word "miscellaneous" today. The synonyms for it are mixed, varied, assorted, and motley. Mrs. Hanson made us look it up along with all our other words, like always. We can use the computer or the big

dictionary that sits on its own stand up by her desk. I
always use the dictionary. I like its tissuey pages and tiny
little print. It's more interesting than the computer.

That was true, even though I was almost the only one who thought so. But I liked how you might be looking up *miscellaneous* when your eye strayed across to something else, like *mirza*, which is a royal prince in Persia, or *miscreant*, which means depraved or villainous, or *mirth* and all its synonyms: *gaiety, glee, hilarity, merriment, rejoicing, jollity, joviality, amusement, laughter.* I went on telling Grammy,

"Miscellaneous" is a word with a long history. It's from
a Latin word, "miscere," which means to mix. You probably
already know that.

Grammy always told me, "'Latin is a dead language, dead as it can be; first it killed the Romans and now it's killing me.'" She said that, but then she made me learn a little here and there, because she said Latin was the root our English language sprang from, like a big tree growing from a seed. Because she was a teacher in her youth, that was the kind of thing Grammy always came up with.

I have some miscellaneous news. The kitten I gave to
Ivy is growing into his feet and he has learned to fetch,

which makes Ivy proud. He'll only do it for her, though.
I'm convinced Ezekiel lays the most eggs because she's
the biggest, but I can't really be sure. Bootstrap is always
trying to fly off into the maple tree. It's true what I read,
that Rhode Island Reds are full of antics. Bootstrap is,
anyway. I'm thinking of getting some more chicks next
spring, but I'm not sure. When you're in business, you have
to look ahead and keep improving, but you don't want to
get too big, too fast either. It's not so easy to bring new
chickens into the coop—it upsets the order of the ones
you already have.

   That's just like school. But the kids are getting used
to me. They don't tease much anymore, and Ivy and
I even sit with some other kids at lunch now. They're
named Charlie and Sasha. We like them fine but we still
like each other best. Mama and Daddy send their love.
I'm trying to be patient, like you said, but I still want to
bring Ivy home with me.

                    Love,
                    your favorite granddaughter,
                    Prairie Evers

Then I put a big smiley face and a bunch of x's and o's.

Grammy wrote back and said she was still keeping Ivy in her
thoughts and prayers, and ever would be. She said it seemed

like I wasn't finding school to be too much of a burden, and I reckoned she was right. It turned out I didn't mind it much after I had Ivy as my friend. Also I did like the swimming pool (and Mama was nice enough not to say "I told you so" about it). I liked learning, too, but that was something I had always done, with or without school. And I liked finding out all the places where the schoolbooks didn't say everything they should have.

For example, they didn't say much in our history book about what happened to the Cherokees or other Indian nations. One day I raised my hand and said I thought they should. Mrs. Hanson said, "That's a good point. There's not room in the book to cover anything in much depth, but we could learn more on our own. How about I elect you my deputy. You look into it and get back to us. In fact, I think maybe everyone should do a little extra research on some part of history they're interested in."

The whole class groaned, but I felt sort of proud of myself anyway.

Ivy waved her hand and said, "The book never says anything at all about the Cherokees who *didn't* get rounded up and sent to Oklahoma. Why doesn't it?"

"That's a good question too. It's the same answer, I think—so much history, so little time. I want you and Prairie to research this together and present your findings to the class."

She gave us a little wink. I saw we had been snookered in a way, but I didn't mind. I knew she'd make sure the other kids listened when we presented our findings, and would pose them a quiz afterward to make sure their attention didn't wander. Ivy was smiling. She knew we had been snookered too, and she didn't mind either. We'd come a long way, me and Ivy, since I first began in school.

IVY'S IDEA

Even I didn't realize how far we'd come until Ivy came up with a brilliant idea. She made me take half the credit, but it was all her doing.

It started with that assignment Mrs. Hanson gave us. The next day after school we went to the library and delved into the subject while we waited for Mama to finish at the Arts Center.

"Prairie. C'mere," Ivy hissed after we'd been looking things up for a while. She was sitting at a computer and I was looking at a book in the history section.

I went to see what she wanted. "Look—it's the Cherokee word for coyote. *Wa-ya.*" She was pointing at the computer screen and sure enough, there was a Cherokee-English translation page.

I peered at the screen. "Look up something else. Look up *friend.*"

Ivy typed in *friend* and hit enter. *U-na-li* flashed up in the answer box. "*U-na-li,*" we both whispered at the same time and then started giggling.

The librarian shot us a warning look and we quieted down. We couldn't stop looking up words, though. We looked up *pencil, computer, chicken* (ruffed grouse was as close as we could get on that). After a while Ivy said, "We should make this part of our presentation. We should label stuff all over the room with the Cherokee word for it."

I stared at her. "That's a good idea."

"We could have a Cherokee word day every day for a week. For a *month*, even. All that day everybody'd have to use the Cherokee word instead of the English one."

"Wow. That's a *really* good idea."

Ivy was nodding. "Yeah. It is. It'll be cool. I bet Mrs. Hanson'll like it." She dragged a notebook out of her satchel and fished around for a pencil, then opened to a new page. "*Wa-ya*, coyote" she wrote at the top, then skipped a line and wrote "*U-na-li*, friend." She punched in more words and found the translation and wrote those down. I hated to bring up the thought I'd just had, but I decided I'd better.

"Umm, I think you're right, I think Mrs. Hanson will like it. But what about—everybody else? Won't they think it's stupid? Won't it just—make things worse?"

Ivy was giving me a look. A skeptical look. "Well, sure, maybe," she said when I trailed off. "But really, Prairie. Who cares?"

GEORGE

The good news was, Mrs. Hanson did like our idea and instituted Cherokee Word Day right away. She said we'd do a word a week for the rest of the school year, and it'd be our job to provide the words.

The bad news was, George and Ivy's mama had become inseparable, like they were joined at the hip. Ivy was all in a dither. I didn't blame her. She was sure George would propose to her mama and her mama would say yes.

In one way it was all right because after George

came along, Ivy's mama was in a better mood. She didn't pay any more mind to Ivy than ever, and maybe less, but her spirits were brighter. But Ivy was afraid they would get married and move to George's place in Poughkeepsie, back where Ivy and her mama came from.

I couldn't deny this would be a serious thing. I wrote Grammy of it right away and began checking the mailbox every day for an answer.

32

BATTLESHIP

I went to Ivy's after school one day when Mama was going to be late getting home from the Arts Center and Daddy had gone to see a man about buying some honeybees.

"My mom probably won't be home even though she said she would be," Ivy told me as we walked to her house. "She almost never is since George came along. And George doesn't like kids. I can tell that if he could get rid of me, he would. Him and my mom both."

She looked very bitter. I said, "Oh, I don't think so, Ivy. I think your mama's just excited about being in love."

I said that, but I wasn't sure I believed it.

When we got in the house, we went to her room and played Battleship. It's hard to play right—that game is not new and Ivy doesn't have all the ships or pegs to go into them to sink them anymore. But it was her favorite, so that's what we played. After a while, the front door slammed. I didn't think much of it, but Ivy altered. There was a different feeling in the air, that electric feeling of a storm coming on.

There was the sound of a chair shoved across the floor and then the bang of dishes slamming in the sink. Then Ivy's mama came to the bedroom door and flung it open. Ivy scrambled up from where we sat and was halfway to the door as her mama was yelling about the dishes not being done and the house being all sorts of a mess and Ivy having me over to play when she had chores to do.

Ivy said, "All you care about is George."

"I'm the adult here, I'll do as I like. George makes me happy, and I guess I deserve a little happiness."

"He doesn't even like me."

"Well, he likes me, and that's what counts. Nobody's liked me like this since—" For the first time since I'd met her, I felt a stab of sorrow for Ivy's mama. *Since your father died* was what she was going to say.

Time stopped. It was like we were on the tip-top of a triangle.

I wondered what Ivy might say. You couldn't blame her if she lit into her mama. She might say, "You shot him. I saw you. How could you do that? To him or to me? Everything's wrong and always will be and it's all your fault."

But after a long moment, Ivy just said, "Do the dishes and clean up the house your own self. I'm always the one cleaning. I bet George wouldn't like you if he knew how sloppy you were. He'll find out the truth about you, just wait. He won't like you anymore then."

Ivy's mama slapped Ivy's cheek.

I jumped.

Ivy's eyes filled with tears.

Mrs. Blake looked as shocked as I felt. Her hand reached out as if to smooth over the slapped place on Ivy's face. But then she drew back. "Ivy, you are grounded," she said. "Prairie, get your things. I'll drive you home."

EAVESDROPPING

I went to the Miss New Paltz Diner alone after school a few days later while Mama was shopping. Ivy couldn't go because her mama had not taken it back about being grounded.

The group of gossiping ladies was there again, drinking their coffee. Anne Oliver gave me a disgruntled look, but I didn't give her any kind of look at all. I climbed up on my stool and ordered my malt from Lolly, and listened to them go on and on. It wasn't very interesting at first, but then Anne Oliver said, "That Tracy Blake is a piece of bad business. She doesn't pay five minutes' attention to that girl of hers."

Another lady said, "You know what happened back in Poughkeepsie. Those people, I'll tell you what. I'll be glad to see the last of them."

The soft-voiced lady named Erma said, "None of it's the child's fault."

"Blood will tell," Anne Oliver answered in a warning tone.

The quiet lady said, "Nonsense. That girl is as nice as can be, I met her when I worked as an aide in the library. Someone did something right. Probably her aunt Connie. She was a decent woman. And maybe even her mother and dad, some ways. We don't know."

"Oh, please!" Anne Oliver said. "That is just carrying kindness too far. The woman shot her own husband."

"I know," Erma said sadly. "But we were never in her shoes."

"Well, I'm *certainly* glad I wasn't in his shoes," Anne Oliver said pertly, and for once I had to agree with her.

"She is not a happy woman," Erma said.

Another voice said, "Could've fooled me. She's marrying that guy from Poughkeepsie and moving over there. She told me so herself when I ran into her at the supermarket the other day. She was talking a mile a minute about it, and believe me, I never asked. You won't be seeing them around here anymore."

"Good riddance," Anne Oliver said. "And mark my words, that child hasn't got a snowball's chance."

She sounded so sure of herself, I couldn't help but believe her. All of a sudden I knew that Ivy was doomed. Terrible things were always going to happen to her, and neither one of us would be able to do anything about it.

I hightailed it out of there then. I went and found Mama at the grocery store and pestered her to hurry up and finish her shopping, and as soon as we got home I pulled out my notebook and wrote to Grammy and told her everything I had heard and everything I feared.

I also spilled it all to Mama and Daddy at supper. I decided four heads were better than one and I dearly hoped they would think of a solution, for George doesn't like children and Ivy's mama is no better, maybe worse.

PLANS
A, B AND C

Mama and Daddy listened close and said they would not mind having Ivy come live with us. But Daddy said, "It's not so easy. Folks don't just give their kids away."

"They might. Mrs. Blake and George don't like Ivy."

Mama and Daddy looked troubled but Mama assured me, "It just is not that simple. I don't think it's that Mrs. Blake doesn't care for Ivy. I just don't think she's very good at it. She's all mixed up, chicklet. She doesn't really care for herself, is more what it is."

"Well, that doesn't do Ivy any good."

Mama sighed and Daddy lit up a cigarette, which he mostly never did in the house. I went over and poked his leg, and he patted my head. It was the same as ever—me nagging, him putting me off. But then after a second he did stub his cigarette out in the ashtray. I looked at him real surprised and he smiled kind of crooked and sad at me.

Later on I was in my bed but not yet asleep and I could hear them talking down in the living room. I heard Mama's voice murmur something real low and Daddy said, "She's a nice girl, but you know I'm right. Even a woman like Tracy Blake is not going to just let her daughter stay with us permanent."

Mama said something I couldn't make out again, and Daddy said, "Of course she's no trouble. It's her mama I'm thinking of."

Mama spoke for a while. I made out Ivy's name, and Daddy said something with a more hopeful note in his voice. Right about then I drifted off to sleep. I knew they didn't have an answer yet, but I could rest assured they were studying on it.

Plan A was writing to Grammy. Plan B was to get Mama and Daddy thinking. Plan C was to figure out something my own self, but I felt somewhat puny about the chance of that happening.

35

HUMAN NATURE

Ivy's mama didn't unground her for two weeks. The situation was desperate. Ivy and I put our heads together at school but we didn't know what to do. It was true. George had asked Mrs. Blake to marry him and she said yes.

They were moving to Poughkeepsie in a month and a half, and nobody ever asked Ivy what she thought or might like. Her mama and George never even said, "I know you will not want to leave your friend Prairie and your school, but I am sure it will work out all right in the end. Don't worry, dear."

To my mind that was the least they could do.

Grammy wrote back straightaway when she received that letter I wrote asking for help. What she said was this:

My dear Prairie,

I thank you for your letter and your faith in me. I have an idea, you can but try it. It comes with no guarantee but if what I know of human nature is true, it might.

What you should do is this. Go to your mama and daddy and enlist them for help. I reckon they will not make any objections. Your mama should go on over to Mrs. Blake's and congratulate her and bring her some small wedding gift like a cake plate or a relish dish. She should be nice as she can be and never let on that she thinks Mrs. Blake is a sorry excuse for a mother.

She should say, "I am just so happy for you. What a wonderful thing love is." And she should say, "I do so admire your courage in moving to Poughkeepsie, such a large city." This is in order to give Ivy's mama an opportunity to rise up above your mama in her own estimation. And then your mama should say, and never give Mrs. Blake an opportunity to speak, "I know how you worry over Ivy and want only what is best for her."

This part is tricky, Prairie, and it is most important, for if your mama overdoes it, Mrs. Blake will feel she is being made fun of and clamp up like a vise. But if your mama underdoes it, Mrs. Blake will not get the point. However, your mama is clever and quick, I believe she will do all right.

Then she might say, "I imagine you are sorely troubled at the thought of Ivy up and switching her schools midyear, but there is no help for it, of course she must go along with you to Poughkeepsie and get registered there, and get all new books and teachers, and have you go along with her to get it all straightened away, and then she must make her way as best she can. I imagine in a larger city they will have ever so many meetings for the parent to go to with the student, and after-school activities that Ivy will like to be involved in. Oh, it will be so much work for you!"

Then she must add, "I am certain it must be a weight on your mind, this upset in Ivy's schooling. And I do not know what my daughter will do. Without Ivy she will be lost. We are only simple country people after all, and Prairie has never gone to school before. Ivy has been a true compass in helping Prairie make her way around."

I know, dear, that you and Ivy are simply the best of friends and all of this other is nonsense, but it is important for Mrs. Blake to have the way all smoothed down for her. Then your mama might say, all in a rush, "Oh, Mrs. Blake, I have just had such an idea. Could you see clear to letting your Ivy stay with us through the school year, just while you and George get settled? After all, you do deserve that, to have that time alone together, and Ivy would be such a reassurance to Prairie. Why, this would soothe all your cares and concerns over upsetting Ivy's school year. She could come to you, of course, on weekends and holidays if you and George are free, but you would be doing us such a favor if you would consider it."

This is important, Prairie, that Ivy's mama be made to feel she is doing a favor when really she is just being offered a chance to jump off the hook like a trout that's been caught in a stream and wants nothing more than to go back to its own life with no thought for anyone or anything. Perhaps Mrs. Blake will say yes.

It is my only idea. You give it a try, and tell me how it works out.

Love,
Your grandma,
Patience Evers

NOTHING VENTURED, NOTHING GAINED

I grabbed that letter out of the mailbox and read it on my way up the driveway, and then ran and got Mama and Daddy. I dragged Daddy out of the barn and hustled him into the living room, where Mama was stitching at her sewing machine. "Listen," I said, waving Grammy's letter in the air. I told them everything Grammy had told me.

"Oh, honey," Mama said, taking the letter and reading it over for herself. "I just don't think I can do this."

"Please, Mama! You have to."

"Can you really see me pulling off a stunt like this?"

"Yes!"

Mama smiled sadly. "I appreciate your confidence, but really— I don't see Mrs. Blake's answers necessarily lining up the way we'd want them to. People rarely are that simple when it comes right down to it."

"But you could try, Mama. Couldn't you? Didn't you always tell me 'nothing ventured, nothing gained'? Didn't you always say you can't fail if you don't try?"

"She has a point there, Loren," Daddy said.

"Yeah, I have a point," I said, nodding with excitement because Daddy was on my side. I could see the whole thing in my head. I needed Mama to do this in the worst way. I really did not think Daddy going to talk to Mrs. Blake would be the same. "Please say you'll try. I've been good about school, haven't I? I couldn't see myself going, and didn't believe it would ever work out, but it's okay. I don't mind it anymore. You were right when you told me to give it a chance, just like I might be right about this. Please, Mama. *Please*."

Mama read Grammy's letter again. She tapped her fingertips on the sewing table. She looked over at Daddy, who just lifted his eyebrows. He meant to tell her that it was all up to her, that she was the only one who could decide this particular thing.

"Oh, all right," Mama said all of a sudden. "What the heck. We'll give it a try."

THE INS AND OUTS OF IT

Mama and I discussed it, and we agreed we'd better talk everything over with Ivy. Ivy got permission to come home with me after school that Friday night—finally her mama had relented on the grounding, but really I think she just didn't want to have to stay home with Ivy instead of going bowling with George—and while Mama was fixing supper, she introduced the subject.

Ivy and I were working on our homework at the table, and Mama was fixing a big vat of stew, which required all kinds of chopping and sautéing and stirring. We thought that would be the best way to bring up the topic—if Mama was busy, but a calm sort of busy, and if Ivy and I were busy, but an easy sort of busy too. Plus I knew how Ivy loved to hang around while Mama was cooking—probably because her own mama hardly did it at all.

"So, Ivy," Mama said. She sounded nervous. "Prairie told me you might be moving over to Poughkeepsie pretty soon."

Ivy had been happily marking off answers in her reading workbook, but she stopped short at that. A blank look fell over her. "Yes."

Mama cleared her throat. "Well, now this might be out in left field, but we just had this crazy idea—you tell us what you think—that maybe there'd be some chance your mother would let you finish out the school year here, and stay with us."

Ivy's mouth opened. A look appeared on her face. It was complicated. It wasn't just happy and it wasn't just sad, but a mix of those two.

Mama went on chopping and sautéing and stirring and she explained what we were thinking, and I put my two cents in every now and then too.

We did not exactly tell Ivy the ins and outs of the plan, because that seemed sad and mean—showing too clearly how her mama seemed to us. Mama summed it up by saying, "We'd love to have you come and live with us, at least for the rest of the school year, if that's what you'd like."

IVY'S ANSWER

I held my breath to see what Ivy would say.

"I would like that," she said. "More than anything."

"All I can do is ask your mother. We can only see what she says."

"Okay." Ivy looked nervous.

"Is there a good time? A time when she's—" Mama trailed off.

"She's usually in a good mood on Friday afternoons," Ivy said. "Like today. She and George always go bowling on Friday night, and she loves bowling."

The next Friday afternoon, Mama sent me and Ivy to the Miss New Paltz with enough money for chocolate malts and hamburgers, and she went to see Ivy's mama.

It was agony while we waited. I could only eat half my hamburger and Ivy couldn't get a bite down of hers at all.

THE LONGEST MINUTES IN THE HISTORY OF THE WORLD

It was forty minutes before Mama returned. They were the longest minutes in the history of the world. Finally she came in the door.

She walked up to the counter and put an arm around each of our shoulders. Her voice was calm. "Well, Ivy, I hope you think you can put up with us for the next little while, because your mother said she guesses it would be all right if you finished out the school year here."

"Hooray!" I yelled. "Hooray, hooray, hooray! Isn't it great, Ivy?"

"Yes. It is. It's great."

Her face was smiling, but her eyes were not, and all of a sudden I wished I'd given a little more thought before I belted out those hoorays. It dawned on me that while Ivy did want to stay with us, at the same time she couldn't have exactly wanted her mama to say it was okay. That would be like having your mama say she didn't really want you. I took Ivy's hand then, and gave her a little upside-down smile to show that I understood, even though I was slow about it. I kicked her toe with the toe of my boot. After a moment, Ivy kicked my toe back.

"Well, come on then." Mama was brisk and businesslike. "Pay up for your lunch and let's get home. You two have chickens to feed. And you've got a cat to look after, Ivy. Pup sure does know who his mistress is, he doesn't come when anyone calls but you."

"Okay." The sad look lightened from Ivy's eyes a little. "But—am I moving in with you today then? Or when? What did my mom say?"

Mama hesitated. "Well, your mother and I thought next weekend would be a good time. That would give you—and her—some time to get ready. And to change your mind if you want to."

"I won't change my mind," Ivy said quietly.

Mama nodded. She looked solemn. "You know we'll take you down to Poughkeepsie whenever you want to go. I imagine your mother and George will be up to visit you too."

Ivy was looking straight at my mama with a grown-up expression that gave me some pause. For the time they looked at one another, Ivy was an adult like Mama, and I was not, and I didn't want to be either. "Yes, I suppose they might," Ivy said.

Mama nodded. She put her arm around Ivy and steered her toward the door.

Just as I was turning around from paying our bill, the nice one of the coffee-drinking ladies got up too and followed Mama.

"Loren? I've been wanting to say hello to you."

Mama frowned with her forehead furrowed. Her hand was still on Ivy's shoulder, and Ivy was looking up at her anxiously. I knew what Ivy was thinking. She was hoping this woman wasn't going to try and get all the particulars of the Blakes' lives right there on the spot. "I'm sorry," Mama said. "I don't think I remember you."

"Oh, that's all right. I'm Erma Phillips. We were your neighbors for a while when you were growing up. My husband had the idea he was going to raise horses, and we bought a place out along your road. Your mother brought over a casserole the first day we moved in, and I was so grateful. She was a good neighbor."

Mama smiled sadly. "Yes."

"I tried to sell Tupperware to make a little extra money after we first moved out there. Your mother always came to the parties and found something to buy. And then my husband died— it was so unexpected—and no one could've been kinder than your mother. I spent more than one afternoon at her kitchen table crying before you got home from school. I thought a lot of her."

"Thank you," Mama said, stroking Ivy's hair. "I wish I'd have appreciated her better when I was younger. I was a little wild, I guess."

"Everyone goes through that," Erma said kindly, and I thought there was hope for her after all. "It's nice to have you back. I hope you're planning on staying."

"Thank you. We are."

I gave the woman a little smile then, to show I forgave her a little for having such no-account friends, and she smiled back at me and nodded as if she understood.

40

THE AIR DURING A THUNDERSTORM

Ivy and I decided right away to share my room, even though Ivy could've taken the one that was Grammy's. It seemed more cozy to us that way. More like sisters is how I thought of it. Ivy's bed was a twin just like mine. Daddy wedged it in between the wall and the dresser the day Ivy moved in. It just barely fit, but we liked it that way. It made it easy to talk softly in the dark about the day just finished or the one coming up. It was like a slumber party every day of the week. There wasn't room for anything but our beds and dressers—I even had to move my bookcase into the hall—but I loved having someone to share the upstairs with me again.

One night when it was storming, with big crashes of thunder and bolts of lightning, I sat propped up in my bed with a book, thinking extra hard of Grammy. She always did love a storm so. I looked over at Ivy, but she was busy scribbling in the notebook she had taken to carrying everywhere with her.

"What are you doing?" I asked.

Ivy looked at me as if I weren't very bright. "I'm writing."

"I can see *that*. What are you writing?"

"It's just something your grammy said I might like to do. She said it's something she does. Writes down the things that are in her mind, and the things that happen."

"What do you mean happen? Nothing really does what you could call *happen* in Vine's Cove." I felt kind of cranky suddenly. I knew Grammy had written to Ivy welcoming her to the family, and that Ivy had written back, but I wasn't sure I liked the fact that they wrote back and forth another time.

"Your grammy said it didn't have to be anything special. She said she might write about how the air felt during a thunderstorm. That's what I was doing. Or she might put in a recipe or a song." Ivy fiddled with a tendril of that plant Mama gave her, which sat on the windowsill right next to her bed. "She said it might help me from feeling lonely sometimes."

I wadded up a piece of paper and threw it at her. "How can you be lonely when you're only two feet away?"

She just looked at me and didn't answer.

I let the subject drop, but I still didn't like it. I knew about Grammy's journal keeping, but it wasn't anything I was interested in, so why should Ivy be? We liked all the same things—supposedly. And another thing—Grammy was *my* grammy. And Ivy had *me* to keep her from being lonely. Me and Mama and Daddy and Pup and all the hens and Fiddle. What more did she need?

But I knew in my heart that a person could be lonesome no matter what. Lonesome for what wasn't and never would be.

I didn't mind living in New Paltz anymore; it had become home. But I would always be lonesome for Peabody Mountain and Vine's Cove. And I was happy as anything to have Ivy living with us, but that couldn't stop me from missing Grammy like a sawed-off leg. So I knew very well that a person could feel two ways at once. And I saw how much it meant to Ivy that Grammy set right in to treating her like someone particular and special. I left her alone about her notebook, but it wasn't easy.

A few days later there was a brand-new notebook in the mail from Grammy for each of us. Ivy's was yellow and mine was red.

"Dear chicklet," the letter Grammy sent with mine said,

This is meant to be for anything you want. It's only a ninety-nine-cent loose leaf from Piggly Wiggly, but that doesn't mean it isn't up to whatever job you give it.

I believe it's a good idea to set down the events of your days and the things you notice, those you like and those you don't, both. These things, big and small, make up your life, yours and no one else's. But you don't have to agree with me! You can fill this whole book with tic-tac-toe games if you want. It's your choice. And what Ivy does with hers is her choice. Remember that, my stubborn chicklet!

Love,
Your grandmother,
Patience Evers

I thought about what she'd said. But setting down words end to end in a journal seemed too much like quilting to me. An awful lot of slow, small work. I'd rather be outside with the chickens. Maybe I'd use the notebook to keep track of them.

Even though I'd been in the poultry business for over six months now, I still didn't have much of a bookkeeping system. I could start by writing down all their names, how many eggs I gathered each day and how many I sold, and what I spent on feed. I could even write down some particular thing that struck me each day—like the way Fiddle lifted his head to crow, or the way the sunlight reflected off Miss Emily's feathers, or about the time Harriet panicked when I wore a hat into the henhouse. She flew into a tizzy and sent the whole flock rushing for the corners and bumping into one another. The hat was a big fur hat I found in a trunk that probably belonged to my grandpa Patton. Maybe Harriet thought it was a fox come to eat her.

I was just about to write that on the first page of my notebook when Pup came tearing around the corner and distracted me. I never did get back to it.

FRAGILE/ FRAGILÉ

On Friday, December the third, the FedEx truck pulled up our driveway in the afternoon. Ivy and I ran outside to see why. We figured the driver must be lost. He wasn't, though. He had two big packages with red-and-white FRAGILE/ FRAGILÉ stickers plastered all over them. One was addressed to Miss Ivy Blake and the other to Miss Prairie Evers. They both came from Mrs. Patience Evers, Vine's Cove, North Carolina. We ran to get Mama to sign for them, but she said no, they were ours, we could sign.

We wanted to rip right into the boxes, but Mama said we had to wait until the next day, which was my birthday. I could hardly sleep that night, wondering about them.

The next morning a few snowflakes were tiptoeing down from the sky, which gave me a thrill even though they did melt as soon as they hit the ground. I woke up early and made my way to the living room to look at the boxes some more. Along with those from Grammy, there were also three packages from Mama and Daddy. Two were for me and one was for Ivy, which I thought was nice—I didn't mind sharing my birthday. Daddy was in his recliner reading a book about beekeeping.

"Happy birthday, chicklet," he said.

"Thank you, Daddy." I gazed at the big package from Grammy. What could it be? A giant stuffed panda? A big Chinese kite, already put together? A huge rubber ball for rolling around on?

"Hard to wait?" Daddy asked.

I nodded.

"I expect you'll want pancakes for breakfast."

"Of course!" I always had pancakes with maple syrup for my birthday breakfast. It was a tradition as old as me, so Daddy was just making conversation.

Pretty soon I ran back upstairs and woke Ivy up, then started badgering Mama to get breakfast going. The quicker the day began, the quicker we could open our presents. Finally, when breakfast was over and the dishes were cleared, Mama sent me and Ivy to bring our boxes to the kitchen table and let us tear into them.

First we opened our two matching packages from Mama and Daddy. Mama's eyes were dancing and she held her hand over her mouth to hide her smile. I started grinning as soon as I lifted my gift out. It was a quilt that was solid red corduroy on one side and a red-and-blue calico print on the other: just two big chunks, a back and a front, sewn together.

"What do you think, Prairie Evers? I finally took your advice."

I ran around the table and flung my arms around her waist. "It's perfect."

I turned to look at Ivy and she was running her hands over the sage-green corduroy of her quilt. The calico on the other side was green and dusty rose.

"Do you like it?" Mama asked her.

"It's my favorite colors," Ivy whispered.

"I thought so." They smiled at each other. Then Mama said, "Go on, Prairie, open your other present from us," and I did.

Even though it was in a Redwing boot box, it turned out to be a gift certificate for the Agway. "I love it," I told Daddy, running to give him a hug too. I knew that one was probably his idea.

Next we lit into our presents from Grammy, and mine was something I would never have guessed. It was a banjo, one just the right size for me. I was so excited, words could not express. I had always admired Grammy's playing, and to have her send me this—it was like I had grown up overnight.

It was also like missing her brand-new all over again. It had been too long since I'd heard her voice belting out "Oh Glory, how happy I am." The moment I thought that, my eyes watered up. I hugged the banjo to me and thought how strange life was. Up and down, happy and sad, good and bad, one thing mixed up with another all the time.

Ivy opened her package next, and what Grammy had sent her was a small guitar. "But she never even met me." Ivy's voice was full of wonder and doubt.

"That doesn't matter. You're one of the family."

Grammy didn't send any note or explanation, just a piece of paper with each that had a song on it, with the chords and the notes and the words written out. I did wonder how she meant for us to learn to play from just that little bit of information, but we set out to try anyway. That afternoon we went to the library and found some books and printed off pages from the computer, then headed for home to apply ourselves to the project.

"Do you think this is really possible?" Ivy asked me, laughing as we left the library. The air was sharp and refreshing, like a drink of cold water, and her long hair was blowing in the breeze. "Do you think we could really teach ourselves to play?"

I smiled back at her. I liked how happy she looked. "I don't know for sure. Maybe. Grammy always says that with effort and determination, just about anything's possible."

Ivy skipped over a crack in the sidewalk. "I think she's right. I think we can. Let's try really hard, all right? Let's not give up no matter what."

42

SHE'LL BE COMING 'ROUND THE MOUNTAIN WHEN SHE COMES

One week later, Ivy and I were feeling proud of ourselves. We'd learned enough that the song almost sounded like itself. We played it over so many times that one afternoon Mama finally got a little worn out on it, I guess. She said that since it was such a fine, sunny day, maybe we could take our music outside.

We dragged our chairs out to beside the henhouse

and began our song again, to see how the chickens would like it. They didn't seem to like it much at all. Fiddle fluffed his feathers and stretched out his head and made as if to peck at me. I stood up and loomed over him and looked real menacing; he frowned (I swear a rooster can frown) and rounded up the hens and made off to the other edge of the yard, as far away from us as they could be.

Nonetheless we kept on, singing every verse off the song sheets Grammy sent. "She'll be coming 'round the mountain when she comes," we sang at the tops of our voices. "She'll be coming 'round the mountain when she comes."

Out of the blue, a third voice joined in from off a ways, a voice that was loud and wavery and plain. "She'll be driving six white horses when she comes," that voice belted out like there was no tomorrow. I stopped playing, and Ivy trailed off too. The voice came closer. "She'll be driving six white horses, she'll be driving six white horses, she'll be driving six white horses when she comes."

My jaw gaped open. It couldn't be. It *couldn't*. But it sounded just like Grammy.

GRAMMY

And then, around the corner she came—*my grammy!*—a traveling bag in each hand. I had never been so happy in my whole life as I was at that moment.

She looked so good to me, I could have gobbled her up like a chunk of cake. I don't know how to describe her. She is average tall, with blackish-white hair cut short to keep it out of her way, and an interesting, smiling face that has a sort of squashed-in, wrinkled-apple appearance. She was wearing blue jeans and sneakers and an old red sweatshirt I remembered from way back, with a quilted flannel shirt over the top of it.

"Grammy," I hollered, running to her, my banjo still in one hand. "Grammy, Grammy, Grammy!"

"Prairie Evers," she hollered back, and she took me and that banjo into a big bear hug. After a moment she set me back and looked me over and gave me a grin to let me know she thought I looked all right. And then she said, "And you must be Ivy." Ivy had walked up to within grabbing distance, and Grammy grabbed her and gave her a hug identical to the one she gave me.

Ivy looked bashful, but her arms reached up to go around Grammy's neck.

After that, we dragged Grammy into the house to see Mama, and Mama rang the dinner bell to bring Daddy inside, and we all began to get caught up. Everyone was talking at once and no one let anyone else finish a sentence, and I swear Mama and Daddy were just as tickled and surprised as me.

Grammy said she missed me too much, and couldn't stand having me grow up so far out of her sight. She said she didn't like living with Great-Uncle Tecumseh after all; the space was too small, and he was too set in his ways. She said it was just not the same down home at all, without me and Mama and Daddy. Plus she claimed to have a hankering to experience a winter up north. She said she always did like a white Christmas, and you didn't hardly ever get that down in North Carolina anymore, not even in Vine's Cove. I said as warm as it was it didn't look like we would have a white Christmas in New Paltz either, but Grammy said that was of no consequence.

Most of all, she said, this business of me going to school and making a fine friend like Ivy, and Ivy coming to live with us, had tickled her interest to such a degree that she just couldn't stand to stay there in North Carolina and hear about it in letters but must come to see for herself how it all was. She had caught a bus and ridden it all the way north, all the way to New Paltz, and then hitched a ride to the end of our driveway.

"I wanted to surprise you all. It tickled me to think of giving you such a start. Besides which, you two have got to have someone to teach you how to play those instruments. A book is a help, but it's not the same as a teacher. So here I am. I'm surprised you didn't guess I was coming, after a guitar and a banjo arrived in your living room." Grammy laughed with delight, a little *tee-hee* that I had sorely missed.

44

THE MOST
WONDERFUL TIME
OF THE YEAR

I was so happy to have Grammy home. I
was busy every minute telling her everything that
had happened in the last year that I might not have
remembered to stick into a letter, and making her
tell me everything she could think of about Vine's
Cove and Peabody Mountain that might've been
the least bit different from when I left.

I couldn't wait to get off the bus each day so I

could check and make sure she was really there. It was like my birthday and Christmas combined, every time.

I adore Christmas. It's the most wonderful time of the year. I love Christmas trees and cookies and carols and presents and wrapping paper and decorations and wreaths. I love how the stores and the streets of towns are all dressed up, and people seem happier, like they're wearing their best moods instead of their everyday ones. I love the sound of the Salvation Army volunteers ringing their handbells, reminding everyone to be kind and generous. I love making presents and wrapping them up and hiding them away. This year I had big plans to share it all with Ivy, but to my surprise she just would not get into the spirit of things.

On our first night of winter vacation I couldn't get her to help me string popcorn for the tree. I said, "Ivy, *what* is the matter? You're about as fun as a science test."

"Nothing," she said.

I asked again and she answered the same and we went back and forth that way until finally I got fed up. "Well, I'm going to start in on that project we talked about. Do you want to come?" We were going to make bookmarks out of colored paper and fabric scraps and ribbons and buttons and things and give them out as gifts. I had the idea when I was helping Mama clean up after one of her quilting projects one day.

"No. Not right now."

I couldn't believe it. We'd already talked the whole plan out. "Fine."

I marched up to our room. I slammed the door behind me and started hauling my supplies out and setting them on top of my dresser, but I was getting madder and madder. After about two minutes I marched back to the kitchen, where Ivy was still moping at the table. "Ivy, you are just stubborn and no fun at all. It's like you're trying to spoil Christmas." I had my hands on my hips and was glaring at her, and Ivy did not look any too cheerful herself.

Before either one of us had a chance to say anything else, Mama said, "Prairie, I need your help out in the barn for a minute. Come on, get your coat."

I started to insist on knowing why, but Mama said, "*Now*, Prairie. Not so many questions. It's coming up on Christmas, after all."

I realized it might be a fun secret, so I scooted out the door after her, hauling my coat on as I went.

But when we got outside, it was not a fun secret. Right away Mama said, "Prairie, honey, you have got to think before you speak."

"What do you mean?"

"It's Ivy, sweet pea. You've got to think how she might be feeling."

"Happy! Or she *ought* to be. She's here with us and it's Christmas vacation, and Grammy's home and everything."

"It's almost Christmas," Mama said patiently, "and your family's all around you, but her mama has hardly even called since she's been here."

I bit my lip. Good riddance was how I thought of Ivy's mama. But maybe Ivy didn't think of it quite that way. Probably she didn't.

"She hasn't asked for Ivy to come to Poughkeepsie except that one time."

I looked down at the toes of my boots. Ivy had gone to Poughkeepsie at Thanksgiving, but George and her mama brought her back on Saturday instead of Sunday. They said something had come up. Ivy didn't say much about it. I thought maybe she didn't mind and was just glad to be home. But maybe there was more to it than that.

"So far they haven't even asked her to come for Christmas Day."

I started to say, *Who'd want to spend Christmas with them, anyway?* but then I said, "Oh," instead.

"That feels bad to Ivy."

"Has she said something to you?" A big suspicious feeling swarmed over me. I didn't like the idea of Ivy talking to Mama before me.

Mama sighed. "No. Not a word. But really, Prairie—how else could it feel?"

The fact settled on me hard: she was right. I should have

thought of it myself. I don't know why I'm so dumb some-times. I don't mean to be.

I went back inside and I gave Ivy a little smile, even though I still felt mad. Not mad *at* her so much as just mad in general. I didn't want Christmas to be complicated. I just wanted every-one to be happy. "I'm sorry I got so crabby."

Ivy shrugged.

"Do you want to go work on those bookmarks?" I whispered, hoping she would just say yes and we wouldn't have to fight anymore.

"No, you go. It was your idea anyway. I don't want to steal it."

"I don't care about that!"

She gave me a real smile then, though it was still kind of sad. "You go start. I'll come in a minute, maybe. I want to finish my homework."

"It's not due until we go back to school after New Year's!"

Ivy shrugged. I sighed and went to make my bookmarks.

I laid everything out on the floor and got started. I got real involved and forgot about everything but what color I was going to put where, and what button and what ribbon. I saw how Mama could enjoy quilt making, but I was glad the book-marks didn't take too long. After a while I realized Ivy never had come in. I padded back to the kitchen to see where she was, and she and Mama were at the oven, pulling a tray of cookies out.

I felt kind of funny. Why were they making cookies without me? But Ivy looked happy finally, just as happy as I'd been wanting her to be. That made *me* happy. After a second I turned and tiptoed away, back to my bookmark project.

SLOWPOKE

By the time I went to bed, I felt good and sweet, like you're supposed to at Christmas. But try as I might, it didn't keep on like that.

Even though we had two weeks off from school and acres of time to play in and all kinds of Christmas things to do and nothing but fun to be had in every direction, Ivy was pretty often quiet and far off. It seemed like everything we said to each other came out wrong, and instead of getting along like peanut butter and jelly, we were all pins and needles, poking each other no matter how we tried not to.

Christmas came and went so fast, I couldn't believe it. We got all kinds of presents: books and games and a puzzle and a sled and a bunk bed Daddy built for us, and it *snowed*, inches and inches. We got songbooks from Grammy for our guitar and banjo, and she showed us how to play "Jingle Bells" together, which we did until we about drove everyone to distraction.

It was mostly wonderful, but I felt cranky sometimes. Grammy was *my* grammy, but now she was Ivy's too, and it wasn't a hundred percent easy to share her, or Mama and Daddy. Besides which, even though everything was just about perfect—Ivy was with us and we loved her—she seemed so blue. I wanted to fix it, but there was nothing I could grab ahold of to tackle.

I watched Ivy carefully from start to finish a couple of days after Christmas. She was as polite as ever, saying, "Could you pass the butter, please," at breakfast and offering to help Mama with the dishes after supper (and I did sometimes wish she wasn't quite so helpful that way, as it showed up how little I liked to pitch in with the inside chores). She wrote in her notebook and played with Pup and helped feed the chickens and gather the few eggs they were still laying now that winter had come and the days were shorter, but she was so quiet about all of it.

"What's wrong?" I asked one day as we were closing the hen-house gate.

"Nothing." Ivy headed up the path to the house.

"Wait up," I hollered, and she did stop, but she didn't turn around.

I gave her a little push on the shoulder when I caught up to her. "C'mon, tell me."

"There's nothing to tell." She gazed off into the distance.

I frowned and studied her a minute. Then I said, "Come on, let's go up in the tree house."

"I don't want to. It's cold."

"I don't care. *I* want to."

Ivy bit her lip and kept looking off into the distance.

"Don't be a pain. Just go up in the tree with me."

Ivy gave a little sigh, but she followed me up the ladder into the maple tree. It was cold, but not as cold as usual for late December in New York, and we were all bundled up in our winter coats and boots anyway.

When we were up there, we sat swinging our legs over the edge. The chickens were down below us, just like in summer, only now we had to feed them meal and kitchen scraps every day because there wasn't much of anything for them to find in the way of grubs and bugs. I watched them finishing their suppers, and a warm feeling stole over me. I did love my chickens. They always seemed to slow me down if I was feeling snappish. I said again, nicer this time, "What's wrong, Ivy? Please tell me."

"Nothing. I'm all right."

"But you're sad."

Ivy shrugged one shoulder. "I was thinking maybe I should move to Poughkeepsie now that your grammy's here."

"What? Why?"

"Because I'm in the way."

"You are not!"

"I'm like a guest. One who's staying too long."

"You are not!" I hollered. Then I toned my voice down some and said, "You are not a guest. Guests don't wash the supper dishes and feed the chickens and share my room, and they sure don't carry dead mice out for the coyote."

Ivy kind of smiled at that.

"You are not a guest," I repeated again for good measure, very firm.

"I guess."

"Don't you like it here?"

"I like it a lot."

"Do you *want* to go live in Poughkeepsie?"

"No." I could tell by the look on her face that she meant it.

"Do you miss your mama?" I asked real soft. In all the time she'd been with us, I'd never asked her that.

Ivy shook her head again, real slow. "You know, I don't. I feel bad about that. Like a person ought to miss her mother, no matter what. I miss the idea of her sometimes. The idea of a mother who was—more like yours, I guess. But I don't miss my actual mother much. I guess I can't. I can't—let myself."

"Well, as far as I can see, she hasn't made herself real missable."
Ivy made a face.

We sat there side by side, swinging our legs. Every now and then I kicked Ivy's toe real gentle and she kicked back. That was our code: we knew what we meant, even if there were no words for it.

"Sometimes I get tired of never being the one to give anybody anything," Ivy said after a long time. "Look at what you all gave me for Christmas. I didn't have anything for anybody but frosted sugar cookies. And your mom and dad bought everything to make them."

"Those cookies were *good*. I'm rotten at cookies; they always come out wrong, all lumpy and burned and raw at the same time. I couldn't have done what you did. And grown-ups are supposed to buy the ingredients, that's what they do. They bought everything I used to make the bookmarks too. And who wouldn't rather have a cookie than a bookmark?"

Ivy shrugged. I could see she wasn't convinced. "Sometimes I just think I ought to go take my chances with my mom and George. You are all so nice to me, but I don't like being a charity case."

I didn't know what to say. I didn't see it that way, but I didn't know how to get that across to Ivy. Finally I had a thought. I grabbed her hand and said, "The fact is, Ivy, that you gave me something I never had before. And it's something I always wanted. I never told anyone, not even Grammy."

Ivy looked at me with a skeptical lift to her eyebrows. "Oh, and what is that?"

"A friend who was like a sister to me."

I had revealed such a deep, precious secret, I expected Ivy to light up like a firework and fling her arms around me. Instead she looked doubtful. "But we're not sisters."

"Sure we are! We are if we say we are."

"That's not the way it works."

"Sure it is."

"You can't just *decide* to be sisters, that's impossible."

"Sure we can. Haven't we done all kinds of impossible things? Like raise chickens, and increase our egg sales with better advertising, and distract a coyote? Didn't you teach Pup to fetch? Everybody knows you can't teach a cat anything. And weren't we teaching ourselves to play the guitar and banjo before Grammy came home, and what about getting your mama to let you stay here? None of those were things anybody thought could be done. Didn't we get our entire class learning Cherokee? If that's not impossible, I don't know what is. We can be sisters if we want to. Who's going to stop us?"

Ivy looked a little bewildered. "I don't know. You just— can't."

"Yes, you can." I stood up and placed my hand over my heart. "Ivy Blake, I declare you are my sister." Then I shimmied fast down the ladder to the ground. "Betcha can't catch me," I hollered, and ran toward the east pasture.

"Can too," Ivy yelled back, and I heard her scramble down after me.

I ran as fast as I could, but it wasn't half a minute before Ivy caught up and flung herself at me and knocked me down like a bowling pin.

"Ha!" she said. "Slowpoke."

I didn't let her see, but I was smiling. "Slowpoke" is not something a guest says to her hostess, so I knew that Ivy had come around to my way of thinking, or at least was starting to. She started back toward the house, yelling, "Betcha can't catch me!"

I hollered, "Can too," and lit out after her.

46

DOGS AND CATS

I talked to Grammy about the situation with Ivy late that night when we were the only two still awake. "I didn't expect it to ever be hard to have Ivy here," I confessed, leaning up against her where we sat together on the couch, gazing at the tree and its little twinkle lights and shining tinsel. "I thought it would always just be fun."

Grammy chuckled. "You're just finding out what it's like to have a sibling. It's the best thing in the world, but from time to time it's a real headache. Why, you should hear your great-uncle Tecumseh and me. We fight like cats and dogs sometimes. It's like we can't say two right words to each other, and you'd think we were mortal enemies even though either one of us would saw off a hand for the other if we had to."

"Really? I didn't know that."

"Scout's honor."

I snuggled closer in to her. "Me and Ivy don't ever fight *that* bad."

"Someday you might. Or you might not too. Time will tell. But something tells me you'll always be close as born sisters."

I smiled to myself because Grammy had read my heart, just like always.

47

THE OLD SHOE, NUMBER 2

New Year's Eve rolled around, and in a way it was just like the year before. We played Monopoly and ate popcorn and drank RC Colas in glass bottles that Grammy had hauled all the way north with her as a special treat. The hand on the kitchen clock hopped past twelve, we all said, "Happy New Year," and the very next instant Mama and Daddy tromped off to bed, yawning. But now there were three of us at the table.

I won the Monopoly game hands down. I have to say Ivy did not apply herself to managing her real estate at all, and Grammy got purely reckless in her invest-ments. She let that old shoe of hers wander into the very *worst* of financial situations. Then Ivy said, "I'm going to make a list of New Year's resolutions before I go to bed."

I liked that idea, so I said I would too. Grammy said she had a firm rule to only write resolutions in the morning and would wash up the dishes instead. Ivy and I got out the loose-leaf notebooks Grammy had sent us back in the fall and settled down to think.

I licked the tip of my pencil—I do like a pencil to write with, it seems to work along with you better than a pen, and makes that friendly scratchy noise that a pen won't make, nor a com-puter either—but still nothing happened. I tested myself to see if I remembered the last word we did for Cherokee Word of the Day. It was *pencil*, and the Cherokee word for that was— I squinched up my forehead.

"What's wrong with your face?"

"Nothing. I'm trying to remember something. The word for pencil."

"*Di-go-we-lo-di*," Ivy said. She was already back to writing.

I sighed. Nobody keeps their resolutions more than about ten minutes anyway, I said to myself. And anything that you really intend to do you are probably already embarked on. I sat there a long time while Ivy flowed along, writing like there was nothing to it.

"What're you doing?" she asked, looking up at me finally. "Why aren't you writing anything down?"

"I'm *thinking*."

"Oh. Well, don't let me stop you."

"I won't."

Ivy went back to her notebook. I frowned. Then after a minute I grabbed Daddy's new beekeeping magazine and used the spine as a straight edge to make a heavy black line across the top of the page. Above it I put MY FLOCK, in big bold letters. Below it I numbered one to sixteen and printed in the names of each of my chickens, starting off with Fiddle. On the next page I used the magazine edge to make a chart where I could fill in how many eggs I gathered each day and how many I sold.

That's what I was writing. But what I thought in my head as I made my charts was different. I drifted through the year gone by. I remembered Grammy's leaving. It had broken my heart. But that broken heart did begin to mend, just like she told me it would, and now here she was, back again, which proved that some prayers did get answered. I thought of selling Mama's quilt for so much at the farmers' market back in September, and Anne Oliver saying Daddy's birdhouses were overpriced. I remembered how it had seemed like the end of the world the next morning, when Mama and Daddy told me they were sending me to school. But then school ended up being where I met my very best friend, and now here I was, sitting in the kitchen with her like it was no big deal and never could've happened any other way.

Across the table Ivy sighed happily. "I just love New Year's resolutions."

"Not me." I frowned over my egg chart.

"I like the feeling of starting new. Getting a whole new chance."

I was about to tell her that was silly. You could have a new chance any day you wanted, you didn't have to wait for a certain date on the calendar. But then, almost by accident, I kept quiet. Maybe Grammy made a tiny sound. I looked at her, but she was at the sink with her back to us.

Whatever caused it, that pause gave me time to remember: Ivy had her way of looking at things and I had mine. They didn't always have to be the same. And I couldn't blame her for having a soft spot for new beginnings. Come to think of it, maybe I did too. "I guess you're right," I said. "I see what you mean."

Grammy turned from the sink just enough to give me a very quick wink.

I tucked my head back down over my notebook so Ivy wouldn't catch my grin and wonder what it was about. She was happy with her resolution making and I didn't want to distract her. I picked up my pencil again but I didn't go back to my egg chart. Instead, after a long pause, I turned to another new page. At the top I slowly wrote, *The Old Shoe*.

All at once I understood how Mama felt about her quilts.

I saw how she could bear to spend so much time cutting tiny little squares out of fabric and then ever so carefully stitching them together. It was like she said—she saw a pattern in her head, and she had to make it come out into the world somehow. What I saw in my head when Grammy winked at me was our story—the story of how Ivy and Grammy and I came to be in the kitchen together on New Year's Eve, with the Monopoly board still set up and the empty RC Cola bottles standing near it and Mama and Daddy gone to bed already and the smell of popcorn lingering in the air. I thought that what I'd like to do was write it all down, so that I'd never forget how glad I felt right at that very moment. *Just exactly one year ago,* I wrote, my pencil scratching along in its friendly way, *right after midnight on New Year's Eve . . .*

ACKNOWLEDGMENTS

So many people influence the creation of a book. For their contributions to *Prairie Evers,* my thanks to the following:

A student I met many years ago at JKL Bahweting Public School Academy in Sault Ste. Marie, Michigan. His courage and honesty in sharing his story did much to inspire the character of Ivy Blake.

Tanis Erdmann, for her editorial work with me, for encouraging me as a writer, and for seeing the strength in Prairie's story when it was first drafted.

Lisa Snapp and Jean Battle, two of Prairie's earliest fans.

Pamela Grath, for so many things—friendship, philosophy, and such devotion to books and bookselling.

All at the Joy Harris Literary Agency. Particular thanks to Sarah Twombly for offering to help me draw Prairie out on paper more gracefully.

Nancy Paulsen and all at Nancy Paulsen Books who had a hand in sending Prairie out into the world.

Rebecca Fuge and her daughter, Elladiss, who read the book midway through its revisions to see what a kid and a mom would think.

John Henderson, of Ithaca, New York, who agreed out of the blue to consult on everything related to chickens for a total stranger via e-mail. Everything that's correct about chickens is thanks to John, and anything that's wrong is my fault. Thank you for considering so much more than just the technical aspects of poultry keeping, including but not limited to sending me E. B. White's "In Praise of the Hen," helping me make the Agway man a more complex character, pointing out how much home-cooked food might mean to Ivy, and sending various photos and videos of eggs, Agway flyers, chickens and even chicken droppings.

John Battle, for reading the manuscript during its final stages of revisions. I was heartened when a guy who'd never read a middle-grade novel before (possibly not even when he was in a middle grade) ended up loving the story.

Ellen Smith. Thank you for comparing Prairie's experiences to your own of growing up as a girl with Cherokee grandparents, and for finding them in some ways eerily similar.

Ilsa Brink, for doing such beautiful work in designing and maintaining my website.

Stan Bontrager, for endless technical support.

Our crew at the West Bay Diner. In the summer of 2011, my gratitude to Laura Bontrager, Amelia Brubaker, Rebecca Fuge, Jenna Hoop, Emily Lowes, and Kristen Scaife. Thank you for working so hard.

The Airgoods and Guths, who've been so supportive. Special thanks to my mother (who grew up on an egg farm and likes chickens better as artwork than in person) and to my sister. The character of Grammy was born one day when Mariann told me, "Crying don't get the oil changed." Indeed it does not.

My husband, Eric, for reading this book so carefully. Thank you for saying this one will be hard to beat.